FIC Zirpoli, Jane.
Zir
    Roots in the outfield

J283

DATE DUE

MAR 2 4			
NOV 1 8			
FEB 1 5			
FEB 2			
MAR 8			
MAR 2 5			
MAR 2 9			
NOV 8			
MAY 5			

5081

Roots in the Outfield

Jane Zirpoli
ATOS B.L: 3.7
ATOS Points: 4   MG

Roots
in the Outfield

Jane Zirpoli

Houghton Mifflin Company
Boston

Library of Congress Cataloging-in-Publication Data

Zirpoli, Jane
  Roots in the outfield.

  Summary: Criticized by his baseball teammates
for being afraid of the ball, Josh leaves his mother in
San Francisco to live with his father, stepmother,
and stepsister in Milwaukee where he becomes entangled
in a mystery involving his favorite professional player.
  [1. Baseball — Fiction.   2. Stepfamilies — Fiction.
3. Fear — Fiction]   I. Title.
PZ7.Z685Ro   1988   [Fic]   87-33900
ISBN 0-395-45184-1

Printed in the United States of America
AGM 10 9 8 7 6 5 4 3

To my children,
Alfie and Beeper

To my children,
Alfie and Beeper

Roots in the Outfield

1

Crack! The clean, sharp sound of wood on leather shot across the field on a fresh June breeze. *Crack!* The unmistakable sound of a solid hit. A fly ball to the outfield. Or a home run. I'd heard that sound before. When Nick Cutter was at bat. My bat never made that sound.

Crack! The sound yanked me out of my daydream. Please God, don't let that ball be coming to me. But when I looked up, the hard, white bullet was screaming toward right field. If that ball hit me, I was dead. Then my feet felt like someone had glued them to the turf. That's right. I froze.

I watched the ball sail past, drop into right field, roll toward the bushes, and stop dead. "Shoot!" If the ball had rolled *into* the bushes, it would have been an automatic double. Now it could be a home run.

"After it, Josh! Go! Go! What are you waiting for?" The coach's voice sounded far away and very angry.

I ran, picked up the ball, bobbled it, dropped it, picked it up again, and threw it. To third.

"Home! Home! Throw it to home!" I heard my teammates too late. Lou Cannizero from St. Remedius had already rounded third and was on his way to the plate. A home run. The game was over. Wilson lost.

"The sun blinded me." I knew it was lame when I said it, but how else could I excuse single-handedly blowing the most important play of the season? A win would have cinched the play-off. Joe Walker was brushing tears from his eyes. Jimmy Kane was bawling, but Jimmy even cries when he strikes out.

"Sissy!" Nick Cutter glared at me. The team was huddled around Bobby, our coach. Except for me. I was hoping the walk from right field to the bench would never end.

"Did you see him freeze?" Nick's hands were on his hips and he was kicking up little clods of dirt with his cleats. "He lost us the game! I swear, the sissy's scared of the ball!"

The words felt like darts. I blinked back tears.

"That was a real hard hit, Nick." Joe Walker stuck up for me. "You might have froze, too."

Nick shook his head. "No way! Besides, sissy Josh can't throw any better than he can catch, so what difference does it make?"

"Yeah," Jimmy Kane agreed just as I joined the rest of the team.

The coach was trying to talk over the noise. "Okay, everybody. Cut the whining. Just shut up and listen."

I checked to make sure my mother wasn't in the bleachers. She hates it when Bobby tells us to "shut up." She says it isn't polite. She threatens to call Bobby and tell him not to talk to us that way. All I needed was for my mom to call the coach and tell him *that*.

"Josh! Josh Morris, I'm talking to you! What's the matter with you? Are you asleep? Are you deaf? What have you got in your ears, anyway? Cotton? Cement? Bricks?"

Bobby waited for an answer. I tried to think of one. The choices all sounded bad.

"He's got bricks *between* his ears," someone yelled.

"No, mashed potatoes."

"Ha ha! Hot air!" Everybody hooted and laughed.

"My little brother's diapers," Luke Feeny suggested. My teammates howled.

"Shut up!" Bobby screamed it so loud that time, my mother could have heard it down the block. "You've got to wake up, Josh. You're not out there to daydream. You're part of a team. In every play. When you see that the ball is heading to right field, don't freeze. Move behind it. Get your glove up and catch it. Don't stand there like you've grown roots!"

"Yeah, roots." Nick Cutter laughed. "Let's call him Roots from now on. Boot the Root. Boot the Root!"

"Boot the Root!" my teammates chanted. I wanted the field to open up and swallow me.

"Quiet, everybody!" Bobby shouted. "It's not Josh's fault that we lost today. Everybody made mistakes. Luke, your fielding wasn't great, either. Keep that glove down! Listen, you guys, we can still make the play-off if Seton Hall loses to St. Barnabas. So hang in there, and see you all at practice on Tuesday."

2

"Don't sweat it, Josh." After the game Danny and I walked all the way to my house. I couldn't face the car-pool.

Danny and I are best friends. We go to school together every morning and spend nights at each other's houses. Danny had warned me about Nick Cutter's clique.

"After all, you wouldn't really want to pal around with the Broncos." (*Bronco* is a word Danny made up for big shots like Nick Cutter. Danny makes up a lot of good words.) And Danny was right. Only now I didn't have a choice about being friends with those guys. The whole team hated me.

I unlocked my front door and brought in the mail. I do this every day, because my mother works. She's a real estate agent. She's been doing this since my dad moved away. My dad lives about two thousand miles away in another state. He's a professor at the University of Wisconsin. He moved there three years ago. I'm not crazy about the arrangement. But then, I'm not crazy about anything that reminds me that my dad moved. Basically I liked the old arrangement when Mom picked me up after school, took me home, and started cooking dinner. And then Dad came home from work and threw the ball with me in the front yard. Mom would yell to us, "Dinner's getting cold, you two. Get in here." Basically I liked it when "you two" meant me and my dad.

Anyway, now my mom doesn't get home until six o'clock. So I try to go to someone else's house after school, unless I have a friend come home with me. That afternoon, I knew Mom had a fresh batch of Mrs. Fields's cookies waiting in the kitchen. It didn't take more than that to convince Danny to come home with me this time.

We sat at the kitchen table drinking milk, eating the cookies, and talking about the girls in our class. Danny gets real hyper when I call girls "dogs." Dogs are his favorite animals. He says he doesn't see the connection between ugly girls and cute dogs. Danny thinks that cute girls should be called dogs. I say that would get very confusing. Anyway, Danny was talking about how cute dogs were, and I lost track of which kind of dog he was talking about, so I started looking through the mail I'd stacked on the kitchen counter. One of the letters was from my dad. It was addressed to my mom.

I've heard that rule about how you should never open someone else's mail. I've heard it and I've thought, big deal. I mean, who wants to read someone else's dumb old letters anyway? It was one of those rules that are perfectly okay because they don't apply to you. Like no-smoking laws. Everyone makes a big deal about them, but they're fine with me. I don't smoke.

But here was a letter from my dad addressed to my mom. My dad writes to me once a week, but he never writes to my mom. At least, I never see any letters from him to my mom. And all of a sudden, I was just dying to know what was in that letter. I mean, it could have said anything. It could have been a proposal of remarriage, for crying out loud. I just couldn't wait to read that letter, and I had to get rid of Danny to do it.

"Take Magoo," Danny was saying. "Why, if I met a girl as cute as Magoo, I'd call her a dog. Name one girl as cute as Magoo." Magoo is Danny's Sydney silky terrier. In spite of the name, Magoo is a girl. She even wears a polka dot ribbon in her hair to keep it out of her eyes. Personally, I think that's sick. But Danny's right. Magoo is really cute. "Go on, name one. I dare you."

I was about to suggest Noel Richards, just to see what Danny said. In February I had decided that Noel was the prettiest girl in the sixth grade. She sits in front of me in class. I suspected that Danny had a crush on Noel, too, because he was always lending her things. This might have been a good time to find out. But then I decided it would be a mistake. If Danny started on Noel, I'd never get rid of him. And I couldn't wait to read that letter before my mother got home.

"You're right," I said standing up. "Magoo's cuter

than any girl in our class. Well, think I'd better start on my homework. Don't want to miss the Giants game." That was lame. I even pulled out my history book and opened it. Danny didn't budge.

"Except, maybe, Noel Richards," Danny said, then paused and concentrated on the chocolate chips in his cookie. "What do you think?"

So he did have a crush on Noel! I knew I was right. "Noel? You must be kidding! No way. Magoo's much cuter than Noel Richards."

"You think so?"

Great! Now Danny wanted to sit around and discuss it. The letter was making me so curious, I thought I'd burst. And my mom would be home in fifteen minutes.

"Now, Noel is the kind of girl I don't mind calling a dog," Danny continued.

I was getting desperate. I grabbed the bag of Mrs. Fields's cookies, rolled it tightly shut, and stuffed it in a cabinet.

"Holy cow! My mom said I was supposed to save those for company tonight. I forgot."

Danny left a couple of minutes later.

It's funny, the information your average kid can pick up. Last summer, watching "I Love Lucy," I learned how to steam open a letter and then glue it back together so no one can tell it's been opened. Well, I put a little water in the teakettle and got it boiling. Then, when the steam started puffing out, I held the letter over it, just like Lucy did on the show. Presto! The flap started coming loose. Then the teakettle gave a little burp, and the envelope got all wet. I decided to worry about that later. I sat down with the letter.

"Dear Anne," (That was a good start, I thought.) "I was happy to talk to you Friday, and to know that I have your support. As I explained, this is all happening much faster than I expected. The wedding plans are now set for June 15." (Great! I thought. They really are getting back together.) "After that, I'll be away until July 1. Wendy joins us on the fifth." (Who's Wendy, and where's Dad going? I didn't get that part.) "I'm hoping Josh will decide to spend next year with us. In any event, it will be best if he can come out early in July this year. I hope this doesn't interfere with plans you have made for the summer." (Now I was totally confused. If Mom and Dad got married again, and lived together in Wisconsin, of course I'd spend the year there. All of a sudden, I understood the rule about not opening someone else's mail. You can't understand someone else's mail!)

"As I told you, when I met Barbara last fall, I certainly didn't expect to decide to get married so quickly. Barbara's chance for a job at Cornell, however, forced a decision. I've gotten to know Wendy, her daughter, quite well. She's a nice little girl. Eleven years old. Active. She loves ballet and is an A student. She reminds me a lot of Josh. I'm sure they'll get along well."

Holy cow! I had always wondered if it would come

to this. Dad was getting married, but not to Mom. My eyes skimmed the rest of the letter, but I could barely read. Wendy. An A student. Loves ballet. And he thinks she's a lot like me! My own dad said that! I couldn't believe it. It was all too weird for an average kid. How could my parents do these things to me? Then it hit me: God was punishing me. Right then and there, I vowed never again to open someone else's mail.

I folded up the letter and put it back in the envelope. Then I took out the glue. I used too much. It dripped all over the sides and squirted out the ends of the flap. The envelope was still wet. How could I explain that? A sudden rainstorm? She'd never believe it. It was eighty degrees out and sunny. But I didn't care. I stuck the letter on top of the stack of mail, went upstairs to my room, and lay down on my bed. The next thing I knew, Mom was calling me down for dinner.

3

"How'd the game go?" That was all Mom said. The table was set. That's one of *my* jobs. And my mom was smiling.

"Okay. We lost." I checked to see if the stack of mail was still on the kitchen counter. Maybe she hadn't read it yet. The mail was gone. The newspaper was on the counter instead. I saw the headline, "Slug Smith Disappears."

For a few minutes, I forgot all about my dad's letter. Slug Smith is my hero. We have a lot in common: We both love baseball. He plays for the Giants and I root for the Giants. We're both right fielders. We both have birthdays on the twenty-third of the month — his is March and mine's September. He's number 24 and I'm number 25. And we're both interested in baseball cards — he's on them and I collect them. At my latest count I own 9,362 baseball cards, including 31 from the early fifties, and one mint Willie Mays that's got to be worth at least twenty-five dollars. This is not average. Very few eleven-year-olds have such a good collection.

But the coolest thing of all is that Slug Smith and I both live in two states. Slug Smith grew up in Wisconsin and played for the Brewers. Then, right about when my dad moved to Madison, Slug got traded to the Giants. When they interviewed him on Channel 7, he said he guessed he'd just have to live in two states, because his home would always be Milwaukee. So he spends the winter in Wisconsin and the summer in California. Well, I always thought that I was a little weird because I spend the winter in California with my mother, and the summer in Wisconsin with my dad. But when I heard that the greatest outfielder in the major leagues lives in the same two states that I do, I decided it was okay for me, too.

Slug hadn't played much baseball that season though, because of his knee. And he was pretty old for a baseball player. He was thirty-five. There were rumors that this would be his last year in baseball. And I'd read that NBC was considering offering him a big contract as a sportscaster. But how could Slug Smith disappear? I decided to hurry up and eat so I could find out.

Then I saw my mother staring at me, and I remembered the letter. If my mom knew I'd opened it, she'd be very mad. And when my mom's mad, I hear about it. Some kids at school say their moms don't talk to them when they're mad. Are they lucky! My mom talks to me when she's mad. She talks to me a lot. But tonight she was quiet. She'd made a big steak dinner. With baked potatoes and sour cream, green beans, and salad with cucumbers and tiny tomatoes.

My very favorite dinner. And it wasn't even my birthday. No, she must have taken the mail upstairs, but not read it.

I'd had two helpings of steak, both halves of potato, and was finishing my beans, when Mom finally spoke.

"I guess you read Dad's letter, Josh."

I thought I was going to throw up my whole dinner. My stomach turned over and I got real hot. Then I waited for an explosion.

No explosion! She just went right on talking as if we were discussing the weather. Moms are so unpredictable. I can't understand them. But don't get me wrong. That night, I was really glad moms are unpredictable.

"I wish you hadn't tried to glue the envelope closed, though, after you read the letter," she was saying. "The glue got inside the envelope and I practically destroyed the letter getting it out."

"I'm sorry," I mumbled.

"Well, I'm sorry too because I think it would have been better if I had told you myself about your father's plans, instead of your finding out that way." Mom walked around the table and was hugging me.

Then I started to cry. I have to admit it. And the funny thing is that I don't know why I was crying. I hadn't really expected my mother and father to remarry each other. And I didn't really mind my father getting married again. In fact, sometimes I hope my mother will get married again so she'll stop worrying so much about me. And so I won't worry so much about her. I don't know what she's going to do when

I grow up and move away. Finally, I stopped crying and my mother sat back down.

"Is it okay?"

"Yeah," I sniffled. "Except that that Wendy person sounds really yucky. And Dad said she reminded him of me. That's gross!"

That made Mom laugh. "Yes, I can see why you might think so. But I'm sure Barbara and Wendy are nice. At least you have to give them a fair chance before you make up your mind. You know that, don't you?"

"Yeah," I answered, but I wasn't sure if I believed it. "I don't want to stay the whole year with them, though. Just the summer."

"Are you sure? Maybe you should think about it a while."

"I'm definitely, positively sure," I said. "I don't want to leave my friends. And besides, I have to play baseball for the Tigers next year. And I'd miss you. Will that hurt Dad's feelings?" I worry a lot about hurting my parents' feelings.

"No," my mother answered. "But we'll discuss it a little more, before you answer Dad's letter. Now about opening other people's mail . . ."

I didn't want to discuss *that*. So I reached over to the counter for the newspaper, pulled out the sports section, and slid it down into my lap.

"There are some very good reasons for not opening other people's mail . . ."

"I know . . . I know." My eyes skimmed the headlines. "Superstar Missing."

13

"There are things that aren't meant for eleven-year-old boys to read . . ." my mother continued.

"I know . . . I know." How could someone like Slug Smith disappear? Everyone knows Slug Smith. He's a national hero.

"Private things . . ." my mother was still talking. I kept reading.

> Slug Smith walked out of Giants practice yesterday and hasn't been seen since. One hour before game time last night, he called his manager and told him he was retiring from baseball and going away to think things over.

Ha! And last night on TV they said Smith was out with a sprained knee!

> According to Smith's agent, Kevin Stein, Smith had been anxious about his slipping batting average and impending retirement. Furthermore, rumors have been flying that NBC is dissatisfied with Smith's trial performance as a sportscaster for the network. Stein appeared to be as mystified as anyone regarding the whereabouts of the baseball superstar, saying that he had not seen or spoken to Smith for the past three days. Caretakers at Smith's Palo Alto estate are equally mystified by Smith's disappearance. Smith did, however, call his home in Milwaukee from an undisclosed location to assure his staff that he was safe. Sally Ross, Smith's personal secretary, said Smith spoke with her this morning and told her he'd found a "quiet place to do some thinking." He would not disclose where he was.

The article continued with a discussion of who would replace Smith in the line-up.

"Wow!" I put down the paper. My head was spinning. "Did you hear about Slug Smith? He's disappeared. He just walked out of practice. Holy cow!"

Mom was smiling. I can't figure her out. I thought she'd be mad because I hadn't listened to a word she'd said.

"Well, I guess I can't worry too much about you," she sighed. "Your appetite's fine and you're more concerned about Slug Smith and the Giants than you are about your father getting remarried."

That wasn't quite true. But if it made my mother feel better to think so, I decided I'd let her.

4

The next morning I was sitting in class trying to read the label on Noel Richards's behind.

"Earth to Josh Morris. Earth to Josh Morris." Mrs. Hannon is the only teacher who jokes about my daydreaming. That's probably because I get A's on all her math tests. I have never figured out why math is so easy. Or why spelling is so hard. I never get A's on spelling tests.

"Roots can't hear," somebody yelled. The whole class burst out laughing. Word sure travels fast.

"I hear you got faced in math class." Danny stood behind me in the lunch line. "That was tight!" he shook his head sympathetically. "Nick thinks he's so tough calling you Roots. Well, wait till you hear this! My little brother, Henry, went to Nick's little brother's birthday party last weekend. And they had this magician. And he pulled this rabbit out of a hat. You know what? Nick was afraid of the rabbit. It started climbing on him, and he started crying."

"Come on. Nick Cutter wouldn't be afraid of a rabbit. You're making it up."

Danny shoved out his right hand. "Wanna make a bet I am? I swear to God it's true. Henry saw it. Henry doesn't make up stuff like that. Honest."

"You're just trying to make me feel better."

Just then, Nick cut into the milk line right ahead of us.

"Hey! No cuts," I warned.

"What d'you care? Afraid I'll cut your roots?" Nick howled at his own joke.

Danny tapped Nick on the shoulder. "Better watch out, Nick, or I'll sic my pet bunny on you."

"Shut up, weirdo." Nick moved to the end of the line.

My eyes were bulging out of my head. "Nick really is afraid of rabbits! What d'ya know. I mean, you'd think a big kid like that, who's always bragging about how tough and strong he is, could handle a little bunny rabbit."

"Wise up, Josh. Even the Broncos gotta be afraid of something."

It sure is great to have a buddy like Danny.

Right after dismissal, Danny and I headed for Applegate Playground. We shared a raspberry pushup, because Danny lost his quarter trying to get the miniature lighter out of a gumball machine in the supermarket where we stopped on the way.

"I told you it was a waste of money."

17

"It wouldn't have been a waste if it'd worked." Danny kicked the machine and rattled the handle until a few ladies turned around and glared at us.

"Let's get outta here," I said and offered to share the pushup with Danny if he'd quit banging on the machine. "Those things are always a waste of money."

Danny gave the gumball machine one last kick. "Rip-off!"

By the time we reached the playground, it was the fifth inning of the St. Barnabas–Seton Hall game. Seton Hall was winning six to nothing. Most of my teammates were sitting behind the St. Barnabas bench, cheering. It's hard to understand how you can be deadly enemies with guys one week, and cheering them and slapping them on the behind the next. But that's baseball, I guess. Anyway, St. Barnabas was up. Across the field, the Seton Hall rooters sang, "Ay batter, aay batter, batter," every time a St. Barnabas player went to the plate. Chris Michaelson was up at bat. Chris waves the bat at the ball like he is swatting flies. He makes a long, slow circle with the bat. Kinda the way I do.

"Michaelson bats like a girl," Danny whispered in my ear.

Thonk. Somehow Chris connected. Sometimes it happens like that with us slow, deliberate batters. It looks more like the ball hits the bat than the bat hits the ball. Anyway, the ball popped up right between the pitcher and the catcher. They bumped into each other and fell down. Then the ball scooted through the shortstop's legs, and the outfielder slipped before he got near it. Chris got to third.

It's a funny thing about baseball. Mistakes are contagious. Teams never just make one. Someone drops the ball, then the next guy throws it to the wrong base. Then people trip over each other and fall down, or run into walls. Things can go downhill very fast in a baseball game.

Well, that sure is what happened to Seton Hall. By the end of the inning, St. Barnabas was ahead seven to six. Seton Hall struck out in order in the sixth inning, and the Wilson Tigers were in the play-off.

Nick Cutter and Luke ran over to me and patted me on the back. For a minute, I actually thought they'd forgotten about my mess-up on Monday.

"By the way," Nick whispered in my ear. "The play-off's been postponed until five o'clock on Friday. Don't forget. Not three o'clock. Five o'clock."

"I won't forget. Don't worry," I answered as Nick slapped me five.

Was I happy! Once Wilson won the play-off, no one would remember anything else.

5

The morning of the Seton Hall play-off, I woke up at five-thirty. This happens to me a lot during baseball season. On the morning of a game, I wake up real early, and then I can't get back to sleep. I get out of bed and pace around my bedroom a little while. Then I get out my uniform. Sometimes I put it on just to make sure I have everything: shirt, pants, socks, stirrups, cleats, cap, glove. There's a lot to remember. Then I practice a few swings with my bat. By that time, I've made enough noise to wake up my mother.

"For crying out loud, Josh, it's six o'clock," Mom calls from her room. "What on earth are you doing? Go back to bed."

But I can't. You see, on the morning of a big game, I wake up early because I get very nervous. And since the Seton Hall play-off was the biggest game I'd ever played, by six I was a wreck.

So I went into the kitchen and started to make breakfast. I guess Mom smelled the eggs or something. I barely got them cracked when she was in the kitchen, too, yawning and telling me to stop making a mess. Mom finished making me a huge breakfast of eggs, toast, and cereal. But I was so nervous, I couldn't eat it.

So I changed back into my school clothes and crammed my uniform and glove into my backpack. Then I walked to Danny's house. It was barely seven, but Danny's grandmother, Nonni, is always up. She was sitting in the breakfast room with a big bowl of coffee. I don't think she ever sleeps — except maybe in the afternoon, like a cat.

Pretty soon the rest of the family came downstairs. Nonni made pancakes and bacon for everybody. It looked and smelled great. Suddenly I got my appetite back.

All day at school, people were really hyper. Especially the guys on the team. We were all nervous about the game. And the hours were dragging. It's amazing how slow time goes by when it's early and how fast it goes by when it's late.

Finally, it was 2:45 and the bell rang for dismissal. Most of the Tigers ran down to the bus stop. I figured they were going to practice for a while. I ran after them and called twice for them to wait up, but nobody did. Then Noel Richards skipped over to me. She was smiling at me like I was the only person in the world.

"Doing anything after school today?" She made a face like she was going to ask me a huge favor.

"Well, the big game against Seton Hall is this afternoon, but not until later. What do you need?"

"Josh." She looked desperate. "My book report on *Sounder* is due tomorrow and I haven't finished the book yet. I know you read it. I thought maybe you could, well, just tell me how it ends. You know, so I can write the report. I'm going to finish the book. I really am. It's just that, well, if you told me a little about it, it would go much faster. We could get some ice cream and talk about it. Please?"

How could I refuse? I mean, she said she was going to finish the book anyway, so it wasn't like cheating, exactly. And it was very hot. The ice cream part was hard to pass up.

"Okay. I'll tell you what happens if you promise to finish the book yourself." I'm particular about people doing their own homework. I usually don't even tell Danny how the reading assignments end, and he asks me all the time.

"We can stop at Baskin-Robbins," I added. "It's on the way to the playground. Maybe you'd like to stay and watch the game afterward."

"Maybe," Noel said. Then she giggled.

I have to admit, Noel didn't seem very interested in the ending of *Sounder*. In fact, I don't think she'd even read the *beginning*. And she didn't write anything down. That should have been a clue.

By quarter past four I'd been through the whole plot twice, and Noel still couldn't write a book report. I mean, she didn't even know that Sounder was a dog. I was disgusted. And I'd finished my root beer float.

"Look, Noel. Good luck on the report, but I've got to get to the game."

Noel looked at her watch. "But it's not till five, remember?"

"How do you know?" I wondered why she suddenly knew so much about that game.

Just then, Jenny Sinton raced into the ice cream parlor.

"Noel, how could you!" She glared at Noel. "Josh, you dummy, what's the matter with you? Didn't you realize Nick was teasing you about the game time being changed? It's the fifth inning. We're losing four to five. And Bobby is so mad at Nick Cutter he just threw him out of the game.

I ran down to Applegate Playground as fast as my legs would carry me.

6

Bobby sure was mad! He was waiting for me with his hands on his hips. And I swear, he was blowing smoke out of his ears.

"Josh Morris, don't you ever take anything for granted about a baseball game again. What Nick did was inexcusable, and I've benched him for it for the rest of the game. But next time, if someone tells you there's a change in schedule, you call me. Get it? You check it out yourself. This kind of thing should never, never happen."

I nodded, pulled on my T-shirt, pulled my pants over my jeans (it felt kind of funny but I couldn't change right there in front of everybody), and put on my cleats. Bobby sent me out to right field to replace Joe Walker, who took over Nick's spot at first base. It was the top of the sixth.

The first batter struck out. The second batter hit a line drive to left field and got to first. The third batter hit the ball right to our pitcher, who caught it for the second out. Then Brian McMonagle came up to bat. Brian is about the size of a fifteen-year-old. Actually,

I think Brian *is* fifteen. Seton Hall pays him to stay in the sixth grade.

Brian swung at the first ball and missed. He was swinging real hard. He wanted a home run so bad he could taste it. On the second pitch, the ball just caught the tip of the bat. Up, up it went. Then down, down, and it was coming straight to me. The sun really was in my eyes this time, and boy was I scared. I shut my eyes, planted my feet in the ground, and lifted up my glove. Please, please, God, I prayed, let the ball be there. And all of a sudden, I felt a weight in my glove. I'd caught it. Out three!

The spectators stood and cheered as we ran back to our bench. "Way to go, Josh," a girl's voice yelled. Jenny Sinton patted me on the shoulder. "See, I knew I did the right thing when I ran all the way up Walnut Street to get you."

Suddenly, I felt my face get totally hot, like someone had turned on the hot water in my veins. I guess that means I blushed.

The Tigers were still behind. But we had last licks. And we needed only one run to tie up the game. Two to win.

Luke led off with a base hit. Then Joe struck out. Craig Lowry hit the ball, but, running to first, bumped into one of our cheerleaders and got tagged. Bobby almost got thrown out of the game arguing *that* call.

Then it was Nick's turn to bat. He had his helmet on and was warming up.

"Come on, Nick!"

"You gotta do it, Nick. Put it away!"

Everyone was screaming.

Bobby looked at me. He was still mad about the umpire's last call. "You're up, Josh."

"Me?"

"Get on your helmet."

"But what about Nick?" Nick is our all-time best batter. I mean, even I knew we needed Nick Cutter then.

"I told you, Josh." But when he said it again, Bobby looked around at everybody on the team so there'd be no mistake. "Nick is out of the game." Then he glared at Nick. "Take off the helmet, Nick, and sit down or I'll throw you off the *team* too."

All the Tigers were moaning. I thought I was going to faint.

"Josh!" Bobby shouted. "I said get up to bat." Then Bobby walked over to me and lowered his voice. "Take it easy, okay? Just get on base."

I swung way too hard at the first ball and missed. Then I foul-tipped the next two. The third ball was low, and the fourth wide. But the next ball came screaming at me, high and inside. It flew through the air straight for my head. I closed my eyes and ducked, raising my bat to protect myself.

Thonk! I couldn't believe the sound. *Thonk!* I opened my eyes just in time to see the ball leave my bat and nail Luke as he ran to third. Then I tripped over the catcher and landed on my back in a cloud of dust.

"Owwwt three!" was the umpire's final call. The game was over.

When the dust cleared, Nick Cutter's angry face loomed over me. "You just had to do it, didn't you? You just had to tell him and wreck the game. Fink!" But Nick wasn't talking to me. He was talking to Jenny Sinton.

In fact, nobody was talking to me. Everyone was screaming at Bobby.

"No fair!"

"You threw the game, Bobby!"

"You let Morris blow the game again, Bobby!"

It was like a revolt or something.

I still didn't know exactly what was happening. I saw Jenny run off the field crying. And I saw Bobby arguing with the umpire. Then Brian McMonagle threw a punch at Luke Feeny. Finally, Bobby, the two umpires, and the Seton Hall coach huddled together on the field. After about three minutes, Bobby turned around.

"Okay, now everybody shut up and listen. There were a few irregularities in this game. We all admit that. As far as the league goes, Seton Hall and St. Remedius play for the championship. However, for purposes of the competition between Seton Hall and Wilson, we will have a rematch September second, right here at Applegate Park."

At first, everyone on the Tigers was quiet. Seton Hall is our arch rival. Nobody liked losing a championship play-off. But losing it to Seton Hall was the worst. At least we had a chance to erase that.

Finally Nick Cutter spoke up. "Okay, Bobby, we'll

have a rematch. But I'll only play on September second on one condition: Morris doesn't play in the game."

My cheeks got boiling hot again.

"Wait a minute, Nick —" but before Bobby could finish, other voices chimed in.

"Yeah, that goes for me, too." Luke walked over to stand next to Nick. "Boot the Root, or I don't play."

"Yeah, get rid of Morris," Jimmy agreed.

"Boot Morris." I even heard Joe Walker say it.

"Boot the Root! Boot the Root!"

The whole team was chanting it. Bobby stared at me helplessly. Then he glared at my teammates.

"Shut up, everybody!" The words rang out over the baseball diamond. It took me a minute to realize that they'd come out of my own mouth. Everyone was quiet.

"You don't have to boot the Root. The Root isn't going to be around next year. Josh Morris is leaving. Josh Morris is moving away to live with his dad in Wisconsin so he doesn't have to see any of your ugly faces anymore. You bunch of . . ."

I was going to say "creeps," but my voice, which had held up pretty well that far, suddenly cracked. Tears squirted out the sides of my eyes, and I turned and ran as fast as I could, hoping nobody saw them.

When I got home, I ran to my room, ripped off my Tigers jersey and kicked it into the corner. Then I threw my glove on top of it. As the glove landed,

I noticed something scrawled on the back. Over my Slug Smith autograph, someone had scratched out "Josh." In its place was written "The Root."

7

"I'm spending the year in Wisconsin," I called downstairs when I heard my mom walk in the front door. I'd decided to write to Dad that night. The problem was, I didn't want to spend a whole year in Wisconsin. But after my speech at Applegate Playground, I figured I was stuck. So I broke the news to Mom right away, while I was still angry. Before I changed my mind.

"Put your coat on. We're going out for pizza, sweetie." Mom hadn't heard me.

When I got downstairs, she realized something was wrong.

"You lost. Oh, Josh, I'm so sorry."

"S'okay," I mumbled, flopping onto the couch.

"You don't look like it's okay."

Sometimes, when you're really sad, it's hard to talk about it with your mother. I mean, I didn't want to tell her that I blew the game. That the kids on the team wouldn't play with me. That they all yelled, "Boot the Root." I didn't want to tell her what a

30

failure I was. She's my mother. She'd take it personally.

"S'okay, really. We'll beat 'em next year." Except I
wouldn't be playing next year.

Mom looked worried. "I know. Bobby yelled 'shut
up' at you again. He's got to stop talking to you boys
that way. I'm going to have to call —"

"Please, Mom, don't call Bobby." I panicked. "The
problem is me. I'm afraid of the ball. I blew the game,
and Nick Cutter says he won't play with me . . ."

We were walking to the car, and Mom had her arm
around my shoulder. All I needed was for Nick Cutter
to see that!

"Well, I'd be afraid of the ball, too. That just shows
you've got sense. If that ball hit you in the face, it
could knock all your teeth out." (Now you see where
I get it.) "One baseball game isn't worth it. And, as
for Nick Cutter, he's just a very rude, mean little boy.
Like his father. Have you heard him scream at the
batters? Nick's a poor sport who's trying to find someone to blame things on."

I ducked out from under my mother's arm. I'd
heard Nick's father all right. And wished my father
were in the bleachers.

Sometimes parents just aren't any help. You know
what I mean? It's not their fault. They just don't get
it. First of all, the whole point of the game is to catch
the ball. Of course it's important. Slug Smith doesn't
worry about his teeth. And second of all, Nick Cutter
might be a rude, mean little boy, but he sure is a good
ballplayer and everyone sure likes him. Parents don't

31

understand things like that. And there's no point trying to explain them either.

"Well, cheer up. I'm not spending money on pizza if you're going to look sad."

"Okay." I tried to smile. When my mom suggests we go out for pizza, I know she means it to be a treat. But I also know it really means she hasn't had time to shop for dinner.

"I guess I was still thinking about that game, Mom. The pizza sounds great. Really great!"

But when we got to the pizzeria, I still wasn't hungry. And I was going to have to tell my mom all over again about spending the year in Wisconsin.

My mom and I have pizza almost once a week now. Every time we order, my mom says the same thing: "I think I'd like mushrooms. But you won't eat mushrooms will you, Josh?"

Now I'd never eaten mushrooms. I mean, a mushroom had never passed between my lips. So I wondered why my mother bothered to ask, every time we ordered, if I would eat mushrooms. She seemed to be hoping that somehow, overnight, I'd decide I loved them.

My mom turned to the waitress, "We'll have one small pizza. Half with mushrooms and half . . ." She turned to me and waited.

"Uh, half pepperoni and green peppers," I answered. The waitress nodded.

"And a Coke," I added.

"Milk?" Mom suggested hopefully.

"Coke," I repeated.

I knew Mom was too tired to argue.

Then I took a deep breath. "I've been thinking about Dad in Wisconsin."

I still haven't figured out how to look when we talk about my father. This is an unbelievably big problem for me. And he moved away three years ago. Anyway, looking happy doesn't work and looking sad doesn't work. There just isn't any solution to this problem. So I always try very hard to make sure there is absolutely no expression on my face at all.

"Oh." My mom sucked in her breath. I saw the expression on *her* face. I was still trying to make sure there was absolutely no expression on mine. So I watched the kid at the next table. He was taking all the pepperoni off his pizza. He picked up each piece of pepperoni and sucked off the cheese and tomato.

"I've been thinking that maybe it would be a good thing to live with him in Wisconsin next year."

"But I thought . . ." It sounded like Mom would cry. "I thought you didn't want to. I don't understand."

If I looked at her I'd cry, too. So I kept watching the kid with the pepperoni pizza. He'd removed every circle of pepperoni and was counting them.

"It's just that, well . . . I miss Dad. You know." I did miss him. That was true. It just wasn't the reason I wanted to move. "I don't want to hurt your feelings, Mom. You understand, don't you? If I'm going to spend a year with Dad, I might as well do it now.

Get it over with. I mean, I'll miss you a lot, but I'll come home for Christmas and Easter. Maybe even Spring Break and Thanksgiving —"

"Wait a minute, honey," Mom interrupted. "This is going to get pretty expensive." Then she paused for a long time. "Oh, Josh, if you really want to be with Dad, of course you can go. And don't worry about me. I'll miss you, but I'll be fine. And of course you can come home for Christmas and Easter, and Spring Break, and even Thanksgiving. You can come home any time you like."

I got up to hug my mom and saw the kid next to me dump all the pepperoni under his chair.

When I got home, I wrote this letter:

"Dear Dad,
I decided to spend the year with you.
Mom says she'll be OK and that she won't
miss me too much.
Also, could you look for some baseball
cards for me? I can't find a Slug Smith
Fleer from when he played with the
Brewers. Thought you might run into one
out there. I prefer mint condition. Did you
know Slug Smith lives in Milwaukee?
Maybe you'll run into him. Ha ha!
Congratulations on your marriage.
Love,
Josh
P.S. Mom says I can come home any time
I want, OK?"

34

After I wrote the letter I went to bed. As I lay there, I kept thinking about the kid in the restaurant. Why would he order a pepperoni pizza if he didn't like pepperoni? It didn't make sense!

8

"Are you really spending the whole year in Wisconsin?" It was the morning of my trip, and Danny still couldn't believe it.

I nodded. I couldn't believe it either. When I decided to spend the year with my dad, July 10 looked so far away that it seemed like it might never come. School wasn't even out; there was a whole month of vacation first, and two major baseball card shows. But July 10 arrived before I knew it! By then, a year in Wisconsin looked like forever.

For some reason, when you decide something yourself, it's a lot harder to change your mind. I don't understand that. I just know that when I wrote to my dad, it was like I'd flipped the switch on a train track. There was no going back. I went through the motions of leaving on remote control. I packed, said my good-byes, and sorted through my baseball cards, deciding what to take. What could I do? My mom was upset enough for both of us. I had to be brave.

The next thing I knew, I was saying good-bye to

Danny, sticking my two suitcases in the trunk, and climbing into the car with my mom to drive to the airport. The drive took almost half an hour, but I don't think my mom and I said more than ten words the whole way. We'd planned everything already: She'd come to Wisconsin for Thanksgiving, and I'd fly out to San Francisco for Christmas and Easter. We'd meet somewhere in between for Spring Break. Then, before we knew it, it would be summer and I'd be "back home." I said "back home" on purpose. I knew that was what Mom wanted to hear. But when I hugged her at the airport, both of us were crying.

Fortunately, once I got on the plane there was no time to worry about leaving home for a year. There were other things to worry about. Don't get me wrong, I like flying. I've flown many times with relatives. I thought it was boring traveling with adults. On this trip, I learned things could be worse than boring.

Now that I'm used to traveling by myself, I know that children board first. But that day, even I was surprised when the flight attendant called out my name ahead of everybody else. It turned out that the only other kid on that flight was a seven-year-old boy. To make things worse, I had to sit next to him.

I don't like to think of myself as a snob, but the worst thing I could have imagined was sitting next to a seven-year-old for four hours. I had absolutely nothing to talk about with a seven-year-old. But there I was. Stuck.

And to make matters even worse, this kid was afraid

of airplanes. By the time I'd listened to the dumb questions he asked the stewardess, I was almost scared of flying myself.

And did this kid love to talk! I took out a book and tried to read. In the sixth grade, our teacher assigned two book reports over the summer. Can you believe that? I say, if it's summer vacation, NO HOMEWORK ALLOWED! But even though I'd be going to school in Wisconsin that fall I promised my mom I'd read the books, and Basil (That was his name. I swear!) wouldn't let me alone for a minute. He wanted to tell me his life story. It was pretty long, considering he was only seven.

After an hour, the stewardess brought us our dinner trays. I think we were the last two people on the airplane to get served. I was so hungry, I complained. And you know what the stewardess said?

"I'm sorry. You and Basil were getting along so famously, I didn't want to interrupt you."

Interrupt us! You mean, interrupt *him*.

"Hey, Joshie (no one, and I mean no one, calls me "Joshie"), look at this."

Somehow, I thought I'd be able to eat in peace.

"Look at what?" I kept staring into my gray plastic plate. The airline had served us a funny chicken leg for dinner. It was fat at one end and didn't have a bone. It had a pink ruffle instead. And it was covered with mushrooms and peas. Yuck! I'd pushed the mushrooms way over to one side, and was trying to pick out the peas. I like peas.

"Watch me eat my peas, Joshie."

"Big deal!" I kept staring into my plate.

"No, watch. Really, Joshie, watch."

Basil had been stuffing his face ever since he got on the plane. It was disgusting. Peanuts, candy, crackers — anything he could get his hands on.

"Don't talk with your mouth full." I figured that would shut him up.

"But I'm not, Joshie. Watch."

I looked up just in time to see Basil cram two peas up his nose.

"Oh my gosh!" I yelled. "That is gross, Basil. That is really, really gross! Now you won't be able to breathe, you dummy."

"Yes I will, Joshie. I always eat peas this way. They slide right down the back of my nose into my stomach. It's neat." Basil smiled at me very smugly, snorted backward and shoved two more peas up each nostril.

Now I've seen some pretty gross things in my time — I've even done some pretty gross things — but this was definitely the all-time grossest. I thought I was going to throw up. I gave up trying to eat my dinner and went back to my book. Just when I found the page where I'd left off, Basil pulled on my sleeve.

"Joshie, I think one's stuck. What do I do?"

"I don't know, dummy. I don't usually eat through my nose." It served him right. The only time I tried to stick food up my nose, my mom sent me to my room for two hours. She said she saw a kid put a crayon up his nose in school. He went to the emergency room and had to have his nose cut open to get it out.

"Joshie, Joshie!" Basil sounded panicky. "I'm not kidding. It's stuck. How'm I going to get it out?"

I looked up. Basil was real red in the face and starting to cry.

"My mom says that when you get food stuck up your nose, they operate." Ha, I thought. That'll teach him.

Boy, was I wrong. I'd no sooner said it, than Basil let out a gurgle. Kind of like a pot boiling over. Then he threw up. All over me. He even had barf coming out of his nose. I guess that took care of the pea.

Well, all four stewardesses ran over. I was so mad. I had my favorite, "U2" T-shirt on. Now it had throw-up all over it. When I stood up, the throw-up dripped down on my new, white turf shoes. Even after the stewardesses took me into that little, tiny kitchen and hosed me down with the sink sprayer, I could smell it. The smell got so bad, I thought I was going to faint. Actually, the woman sitting across the aisle finally did faint, just before we landed. But I was glad about that. At least she couldn't glare at me and Basil anymore.

9

I don't say you should trust first impressions, but, let's face it, first impressions are pretty important. That's why I wanted to make sure I ditched Basil before I got off the plane. It was bad enough meeting my stepmother and stepsister for the first time. I didn't need Basil tagging along. What if Barbara and Wendy saw Basil and thought he was me? Or what if they just thought he was the kind of kid I palled around with? I decided I couldn't risk it. I had to think of a way to stall Basil on the plane while I got off.

"Hey, Basil." We had just touched ground. Basil was leaning so hard against me, he was almost in my lap. "The stewardess said to wait for her before you get off the plane. The pilot wants to talk to you. To congratulate you on being such a great flyer. He's got a prize for you. Whatever you do, don't get out of your seat until you talk to the stewardess."

The plane came to a complete stop at the terminal, and I waved good-bye to Basil. He was still strapped in his seat, smiling happily about the prize he thought he was going to get. I figured that the stewardess would come up with something.

I spotted my dad the minute I walked through the deboarding gate. I hadn't seen him since Christmas. Or since he'd remarried. I didn't know what to expect. Dad's got short brown hair, glasses, and a real thick beard and mustache. He looked the same. "So far, so good," I thought.

"What happened to you, son?" Dad was staring at my shirt. "Run into some bad weather? You're a mess!" Dad hugged me. I was worried he might not hug me with all of Basil's barf on me.

I started to explain about the peas and Basil. Then I looked around.

"What about Barbara and the kid?" My dad was alone. For a second, I thought maybe Barbara and my dad were divorced already. Well, anything's possible.

"Oh, they're waiting outside in the car. It's impossible to park. We're leaving for the lake right from the airport. How's that sound?"

"Great!" The lake just might be my favorite place in the world. It's way up north. About a three-hour drive from Madison.

"When we get your suitcases, you can put on a clean shirt for the trip."

We walked downstairs to the baggage claim. Waiting for the bags is always the hardest part of meeting my dad. I have to catch him up on one whole year of my life. That's not easy when you're getting nailed in the head with somebody's water skis.

First, I check him over to make sure nothing is changed. Fortunately, so far, he's always looked exactly the same. Except for one thing. Every time I see him, he looks shorter. I can't figure it out. I hate to say this, but frankly, I think my dad's shrinking.

Next, I try to tell Dad everything I've done that year. But the words always pile up. Like at Candlestick Park, when forty thousand fans try to get on the field after a game. They get stuck in the aisles.

Finally, I just peek over at Dad every couple of minutes. To make sure he's really there.

Well, to make it worse, after waiting for my bags for twenty minutes, nothing from my flight had appeared. Except Basil! He saw me immediately.

"Joshie, look what the pilot gave me."

Basil was holding out a sleek, silver pen with the insignia of the airline on it. It had a tiny compass on the end of it and a clock on the side.

"That's neat." I tried to sound unimpressed, but I think Basil could tell I was jealous.

"Know what else?"

I didn't want to know.

"The pilot took me into the cockpit and let me work the controls. Is that ever awesome!" *Awesome* was a word I taught Basil on the flight. "You should have stayed and waited for the stewardess, too, Joshie."

I was beginning to think he was right.

Then Basil introduced us to his mother. He didn't have to. It turns out Basil's mother is famous. My dad recognized her immediately. She's on the Madison evening news. And, boy, is she pretty! Have you ever

43

noticed how sometimes really goofy-looking kids have the foxiest-looking mothers? That's weird.

Basil's suitcase was the first one off the carousel. Dad and I stood there while 173 more pieces of luggage slid down the ramp. I counted them. Finally, I saw my black and orange duffel bag teeter on the top of the slide. The duffel bag had the other book I was supposed to read, my toothbrush and comb, underwear, socks, and pajamas. The duffel bag slid slowly down to where Dad and I were standing. Then the carousel stopped. That was it. No more luggage from Flight 624.

It took about an hour for Dad to fill out all the baggage claim forms. I was standing at the airline counter looking over Dad's shoulder. For all anyone knew, my bag was on its way to Anchorage.

"What happens if you don't find it?" As far as I was concerned, the situation was hopeless. Who was going to return a suitcase with a mint Willie Mays baseball card in it, and an entire 1986 mint set of Topps? I couldn't go a whole year without any of my collection. And my Giants baseball hat was in there. The one I got on Cap Day when Slug Smith hit a winning grand slam on a three-two pitch with two out in the bottom of the ninth. My Giants warm-up suit was lost, too. And then I remembered my glove. My Wilson glove. The one I'd spent three days oiling. The one I'd rolled up and kept under my mattress for two weeks until it was just the right shape. The one Slug Smith signed on Autograph Day, the summer of 1985. The one my teammates rededicated to The Root. All of a sudden I started to cry.

"It's all right, son." My dad put his arm around me. "We'll get the suitcase back. You'll see."

But Dad didn't understand.

"If we don't find it, we'll give you fifty dollars to buy some new clothes," the man from the airline said, trying to sound encouraging. "That's not so bad, is it?"

"Fifty dollars!" My voice rang out through the terminal. Didn't they know what a Slug Smith glove was worth? Or a mint Willie Mays? Or a 1986 Topps set? Fifty dollars! Those things are priceless! I guess I got hysterical then.

"He's just a little wrought up over the trip." Dad was pretty embarrassed. "I'm sure you'll do everything you can."

I'd calmed down a little by the time we reached the car. Talk about first impressions! I was still wearing that disgusting shirt, and my face was puffy and streaked from crying. Barbara and Wendy didn't look so great either. It was ninety-five degrees, and they'd been driving around and around the terminal for over an hour.

"Josh, this is Barbara and Wendy. Barbara and Wendy, this is Josh."

I climbed into the back seat of my dad's car. It seemed like no one said another word till we were halfway to the lake.

"P.U. The car smells like throw-up." Wendy was

scrunched up in the far corner of the back seat. The car was really hot, but I couldn't smell anything. I guess I'd gotten used to it.

"There is an odd smell . . ." Barbara agreed hesitantly.

By then I'd had a chance to check out my new relatives. Barbara looked okay. She was wearing a gray jogging suit like the one my mom wears to yoga. And I noticed right away that Barbara is not as good-looking as my mom. Barbara's kind of plain-looking, which, actually, I was glad about. I'd have felt very bad if Barbara was prettier than my mom.

Wendy, on the other hand, was a real dog. I mean, she had her hair pulled back in a doughnut, and she was wearing a T-shirt with ballet shoes on it. Dad told me she'd just come from a "recital."

"It's Josh. P.U., Mom, he smells."

Barbara glanced over at me and smiled. She'd been looking at me and smiling every five seconds. It made me very nervous. I couldn't see anything to smile about.

"That's not nice, Wendy. It's just a bad smell from outside." We were driving through dairy country. "Manure or something."

"Mommie, it's Josh. I know it's Josh."

"Wendy," Barbara said sternly, "you apologize." Then she smiled at me again. "I'm sorry, Josh."

I didn't know what to say.

"It is too Josh."

"It is not, young lady. Be quiet right now or —"

"She's right. It is Josh," my Dad cut in. "Somebody threw up on him on the plane."

"See?" Wendy gloated. "How gross. What'd you do to make them throw up? Smile?"

That was the last thing anyone said till we got to our house on the lake.

So much for first impressions.

10

I was the first one out of the car when it stopped.
There's only one advantage to the airline's losing your
suitcases. If you don't have any suitcases, you don't
have anything to bring in from the car. Right?

Wrong!

"Josh! Where the heck do you think you're going?"

I was around the house and halfway down the dock
by the time I heard my dad. It was early evening. My
favorite time of day at the lake. The sun was setting
over God's Country (God's Country is the name of
the tackle shop where we get our suckers and night
crawlers. I think it's a pretty funny name for a store.
There's a soda fountain there, too. And that year, they
put in video games.), and I didn't want to miss a
second of it. Because when the sun sets over the lake,
it lights up all the windows on the eastern shore like
tiny fires in the trees. The water gets very still. The
loons cry. The dinner gong sounds at Camp Tecumseh on Moose Point. And then the very first bats
dart out of the trees to play, and dive for their supper
of bugs. At sunset, the lake is the quietest, peacefullest,
prettiest place in the world.

"Yeeeeeow!" Wendy screamed so loud, I almost fell off the dock.

"Eeeeeeek!" Her voice echoed across the lake. I bet they heard it all the way to God's Country.

"Yikes!" That was Barbara.

"Josh! Josh! Get over here right this minute." That was my dad again. He sounded really angry.

I ran up the dock. Only half the sun had disappeared behind the trees. Normally, I like to stay for the entire sunset. I like to count how many seconds it takes for the sun to disappear completely, after the highest branch of the tallest pine tree first tickles its underside. It usually takes between 85 and 102 seconds. The best part of the sunset is the last 40 seconds. Then the top of the sun kind of swells over the tree line like a big orange bubble. It swims there a while and grows, so you think it just might not set after all. And then, blip! It's gone. All of a sudden. And you say good-bye to one more summer day.

Anyway, I couldn't stay for the bubbly part, or the blip, because Wendy and Barbara were screaming. And my dad was really mad.

"Josh, come help me!"

I ran round the house and there was Dad staring at this bat caught in his tennis racket.

"Awesome! That's neat! How'd you do that, Dad?"

"I didn't *do* it." Dad didn't think it was awesome at all. "The bat flew out from under the roof and scared Wendy. Barbara swung at the bat with my racket, and now the bat's stuck. Help me find a stick or something to poke it out with."

"That's radical, Dad! Bats never get caught. They're really smart." Out on the lake, I'd seen bats pick bait right off my hook while I was casting.

"Now I know what they mean by 'blind as a bat.' " Barbara was really hyper. "Don't touch it, Ted. It could have rabies."

If Barbara started telling my dad what to do, we were really in trouble! But Dad wasn't mad at Barbara. In fact, he even smiled at her.

Just then, another bat swooped out from under the roof. Wendy screamed again and bit the dust. She had her sweater wrapped around her head. "Ohhh," she wailed. "It'll get tangled in my hair, and I'll have to cut it all off."

"Be quiet, Wendy!" Dad snapped. He was really ticked off with Wendy. About time, I thought. "Bats don't get caught in people's hair. That's an old wives' tale. Bats have very sophisticated radar. They won't come near you. And they don't bump into things."

"Then how come that bat's caught in the tennis racket?" Wendy wasn't at all convinced.

"Tennis rackets are different. The strings interfere with the bat's radar. Bats *do* run into tennis rackets."

Dad's explanation wasn't great. I wondered if I should put my sweater over my head, too. I found a long stick, but Dad couldn't untangle the bat. Finally, he threw the racket down. The bat jiggled free and took off into the woods.

"Wendy." I sounded very cool as I picked up some grocery bags and followed my dad and Barbara into the house. "Bats live all over these woods. If you're afraid of bats, you might as well go home."

Wendy ran past me into the house and up the stairs to the bathroom. "Don't you think I wish I could?" she hollered as she slammed the door.

Just then, it dawned on me that Wendy wasn't happy to be here.

11

When I woke up the next morning, I forgot all about Wendy and Barbara. I jumped out of bed and ran into my dad's room the way I always do. Every morning at the lake I climb into bed with Dad and we decide what we're going to do all day.

Forget that idea. When I opened the door I saw poor Dad scrunched up on a corner of the mattress with his foot hanging out from under the covers. Barbara took up the whole rest of the bed! There certainly wasn't room for me.

So I tried to use the bathroom. Forget that, too! The door was locked. That's right. Wendy. I wondered if she'd spent the whole night in there. I told her it was an emergency.

"Go in the bushes!"

Can you believe hearing that in your own home? They were taking over.

So I put on my shorts and my cruddy T-shirt (I had nothing else to wear) and went outside. When I finished, Wendy was lying on one of the couches in the living room, reading the newspaper. She pretended not to see me. So I went into the kitchen and got my cereal. Then I heard Dad and Barbara.

"Morning, Josh." Dad was standing in the doorway in the same blue terry cloth robe he always wore. But things were definitely different. Barbara stood right behind him smiling. My dad cleared his throat. "Ah . . . Josh. Maybe, from now on, you should knock."

I pretended not to hear him.

"Can I have the sports page?" I asked Wendy. The sports page is something I read every morning. At my house in San Francisco, it's easy. My mom never looks at the sports page. She doesn't have to. If there's anything interesting, I read it to her. "I want to see if they've found out where Slug Smith is." I reached out my hand, but all I got was Wendy's voice.

"They haven't heard a thing. It says here that Smith's manager has 'expressed some concern over Smith's safety.' He's asking the San Francisco Police Department to look into the matter —"

"Hey! Give me that." I couldn't believe it. Wendy had my sports page, too. It was the final straw. I stomped over to the sofa and grabbed the paper out of her hands. "That's mine, you turkey."

"Give it back, creep!"

"Kids. Wait a minute," Dad broke in.

But Wendy had already jumped me from behind. She was really strong. Not strong enough, though. I rolled over and pinned her on the carpet.

"Never take my sports page again. Swear? Swear or I won't let you up. This is my house and my paper."

Wendy was trying really hard not to cry. "I hate your house. I hate you, Josh Morris."

Suddenly my dad grabbed me by the collar. Was he mad. At me! And I thought he'd be proud of me for sticking up for us. It was too confusing for an average kid.

"*Our* house. *Our* paper. It's Wendy's now just as much as it is yours. What's the matter with you, Josh? Apologize. You apologize to Wendy right now."

I ran to my room, buried my head in the pillow, and moaned. I couldn't stand it another minute. And I was stuck with them for a whole year!

When I turned over, Dad and Barbara were standing in the doorway. Barbara was trying to smile, but Dad looked miserable. Good! I thought. I won't apologize. Instead, I rolled over onto my stomach again and spoke into my pillow.

"Ah . . . Dad. Maybe from now on, *you* should knock."

12

Dad must really have felt crummy about our first morning at the lake. The second morning, I heard a knock on my door. Next thing I knew, Dad had crawled under the covers with me.

"What are we going to do today?"

"Who's 'we'?" I asked suspiciously. If "we" meant Wendy and Barbara, I was staying in bed.

"You and me, silly. What shall we do?"

Turtle Lake is the only place where a grown-up will ask a kid, "What are we going to do today?" At home, Mom hates it when I ask her that. But at the lake, parents ask, "What are we going to do today?" and they even sound excited about it.

"Let's go canoeing," I suggested. My dad's got an old, green, wooden canoe. It weighs a ton. "Then let's swim. And then let's take a picnic and do some casting off Ahlstroms' dock."

The Ahlstroms are Maynard and Oscar Ahlstrom. My dad says their house is on the best piece of property on the lake. It's the property right next to ours. But the Ahlstroms' house is on the point, so they have two beaches: a sandy one with a great drop-off for diving, and a rocky one with the best dock on the lake for catching walleye. The Ahlstroms also have a huge clearing, almost a meadow, between the main house and the guesthouse, where I play baseball.

You might wonder why I know so much about the Ahlstroms. Well, that's because Maynard and Oscar are my friends. Maynard and Oscar Ahlstrom were born on Turtle Lake and have lived here — forever, I guess. You could even say they're famous around here. And they let me swim and fish on their property any time I want. In fact, having the Ahlstroms next door is kind of like having two places on the lake.

"The canoeing's a great idea. I'd love to go canoeing." Dad had gotten up and was looking out the window. "Looks like a great day for swimming, too."

"Sure does." I stood beside him. Through the trees, the lake was already shimmering like silvery Christmas tinsel. "Let's get breakfast."

On the way to the kitchen, I noticed Barbara and Wendy were already eating their breakfast together on the deck. That was a good sign. It meant Dad and I could be alone in the kitchen.

We were seated at the breakfast table when Dad turned to me again. "Say, didn't I write to you about the Ahlstroms?"

"About the Ahlstroms?" For a minute, I thought maybe one of the old guys had died. "You didn't write anything. What about them?" Maynard was ninety and Oscar was eighty-five. But they always looked healthier than my dad. I wondered if it was the long, cold winter; maybe it preserved people, like hot dogs in a freezer.

"Oscar and Maynard moved to Arizona this spring. Put the house up for sale. I saw them the morning they left. They said to say good-bye to you. I guess I forgot to write about it."

"Oh." I was awfully glad the Ahlstroms were still alive. "Did they sell the place?"

"It was for sale all winter. They were asking one heck of a price. I looked at the place, too. You know how we've always liked it. They've got a darn good boathouse. Did you know that the Ahlstroms' father built the main house, stone by stone? It's a real beauty. And Maynard built the guesthouse from timber he cut down on the property. Built it all by himself. Said Oscar wouldn't lift a finger to help. 'What do ya be wanting a guesthouse fer?' That's what Maynard claims Oscar said. 'As if two old Swedes would be having guests.' Remember that funny way they talked? And you know, Oscar was right. They never did have a single guest. The place is badly run-down."

"So why didn't you buy it?" Suddenly I realized what my dad was getting at. With the Ahlstroms gone, we might not be able to use the place anymore.

"I'll tell you why. Maynard and Oscar turned out to be two sharp businessmen. They figured Turtle Lake was getting pretty popular. You wouldn't believe the price they were asking. I couldn't begin to afford it. They turned my offer down flat. But I really

57

thought, come next winter, they'd be jumping at it. I didn't think anyone would pay that kind of money for land up here in the middle of nowhere."

"So?"

"So next thing I know, the For Sale sign is down, and Maynard and Oscar are loading up the U-Haul to drive to Arizona. They got every penny they asked for. All cash."

"So who bought it?"

"That's the strange part. They wouldn't say. It's someone very rich. But they wouldn't tell me who. The first thing the new owner did was put a fence around the property. It's too bad. It kind of spoils things. I think it must be some big businessman from Oklahoma. It's odd, though, because I haven't seen a soul over there all summer, except this one sort of strange man. He's never introduced himself. He just roams around the place wearing a torn T-shirt and a cap pulled down over his eyes. I can't imagine *he* could be the owner, though, the way he acts and all. I figure he must be a caretaker the owner pays to make sure no one trespasses. I tried to say hello one day when I saw him on the beach. Thought I might find out who bought the place. But the guy just pretended he didn't see me. Turned around and went back into the woods. Kind of an angry looking fellow." My dad stopped for a minute and took a deep breath. "Naturally, Josh, the reason I'm telling you all this is because I think you'd better not wander over there this time. I mean, it's private property. We may not be welcome. Who knows? Anyway, until I meet the new owner, I want you to stick around here."

Just then, Barbara walked in from the deck. She had her robe on. It was blue plaid, just like the one I lost in my suitcase. "Morning, Josh," she yawned. For the first time she didn't smile at me. In fact, she didn't look at me at all.

Then Wendy waltzed in (and I mean literally waltzed) in her leotard. Stick around here? I thought. Gross!

13

After breakfast, Dad and I charged down to the dock. As we shoved off, I noticed Wendy at the window. She looked really down. I almost yelled back, "Want to come?" but caught myself. Dad and I were alone. Why invite *her* along?

The lake was deserted. The water was so still, it looked like a pane of glass. It was too early in the morning for water skiers. Too late for fishermen. For a few minutes, the lake would belong only to me and my dad. I wasn't going to share him with anybody! I decided to pretend we were explorers, all alone for thousands of miles in the wilderness.

Sometimes, I can make myself believe I'm somebody else. Honestly, I'm that good at pretending. Like when I play the outfield, I pretend I'm the Yankee Clipper. Two out. Bottom of the eighth. "Go Joe! Go Joe!" Three-two fast ball. Grand slam over the left-field fence. The crowd goes wild as I turn third and sprint home.

Well, that morning my faithful Indian guide, Swampscut, and I were paddling the icy border waters on our way to the fort. Our canoe was laden with ermine, bearskin, beaver, and white fox. Suddenly, Swampscut cocks his head. He stiffens, outlined in the morning sun, his paddle inches above the water. "Shh — Josh — over to the right. Don't look now. Don't stare. But there's that guy."

I swung my head around quickly, one foot still in my daydream. I think I half expected to see a Chippewa in full face paint and a war bonnet. Instead, two dark, angry eyes spied on me through the tall grass along the lake shore.

"Josh, I said don't look. That's the man. The strange fellow I told you about."

But just as my father spoke, the man turned away and disappeared into the woods. A shiver ran down my spine.

"Let's get out of here," I said, jamming my oar straight down through the water at the left side of the canoe. My dad paddled right and our boat swung around.

I heard the music all the way down on the dock. Violins, trumpets, flutes, cymbals. Just the kind of music I hate.

"What *is* that racket?" I called back to my dad. The noise was obviously coming from our cabin. It was embarrassing.

"Probably Wendy. She's supposed to be practicing for another recital."

"Another what?"

"Another recital. You know. The dancing."

This was the kid my dad said reminded him of me.

"Well, she's scaring all the birds away," I grumbled, pulling open the screen door. I'd meant the crack to be funny. When I stuck one foot in the living room, I realized I was closer to the truth than I thought. The whole house was shaking. It felt like an earthquake. The furniture had been pushed aside, the hearth rug rolled up in a corner. And Wendy was careening around the living room like a wounded buffalo. It wasn't a pretty sight.

"You're scaring all the animals," I shouted over the din. "Get some earphones or something. You can't blast that noise all over the lake."

Now these are the very words my father had used the summer before when I turned on my Clash tapes. Wendy stopped dancing and glared at me.

Barbara answered without looking up from the sofa where she was reading, "Wendy can't wear headphones while she's dancing. It wouldn't work, Josh. Too much moving around."

I looked smugly at my dad, waiting for him to back me up. Instead, he agreed with Barbara, "Barbara's right, Josh. The music is something we'll all just have to live with."

I guess that was too much for me. I stomped out of the room and slammed the sliding screen shut. It jumped off its track just as it hit the metal siding. This happens every summer. I'm always the one who does it. And every summer my dad has a fit.

"Josh! When will you learn to close the screen gently? Now look what you've done."

But I already knew what I'd done, so I raced down the steps, and I didn't look back till I was around the drive, up the hill, and on the trail across Arrowhead Point.

14

Have you ever noticed how you can be really miserable, I mean kind of dying inside, and life just won't let you enjoy your misery? Like that afternoon at the lake, I was angry at Dad, Barbara, and Wendy, scared because of our weird neighbor, and lonely because I was thousands of miles away from my home and my mom. I had a million reasons to be miserable. I even wanted to be miserable. But life wouldn't let me.

First, the grasshoppers started teasing me, jumping up ten, fifteen feet ahead of me. Big, fat, juicy grasshoppers. Just the kind I like to catch. The kind that burst with tobacco, and spit it in the palm of your hand the minute you cup it over them. But I knew that I had to ignore the grasshoppers. Because once I got started catching them, I'd forget how miserable I was. And I wanted to stay miserable. So I kicked dirt at the grasshoppers and kept on walking up Arrowhead Trail.

Well, if that wasn't enough, next I heard a frog croak. For some reason, there haven't been any frogs at Turtle Lake for over two years. My dad says it's the result of some change in the ecology of the lake. One fall, all the frogs just died. Dead frogs were everywhere. It was revolting. And they never came back. But that afternoon, I distinctly heard a frog croak in the bog bordering the road. I threw a rock in the bog and kept on walking.

All around the bog grew the straightest, furriest cattails I'd ever seen. They even seemed to be waving at me. "Hi, Josh," they seemed to say. "The frogs are back. Come over here and pick me, and poke out a frog or two." But I pretended not to see the cattails, because I knew that if I felt the smooth furry rods, or followed a frog into a bog, I'd forget how miserable I was. And I didn't want to forget.

Soon orange and yellow butterflies were twirling around my head. I found a bird nest. It still had a piece of turquoise blue eggshell inside. The sky was blue too, with just a few cotton balls of clouds on the horizon. And all I wanted was to be miserable. It made me so mad!

Suddenly I was mad at the whole darn world. It just wouldn't leave me alone. I swatted one of the butterflies. It spiraled to the ground. For a minute I thought I'd killed it. Then I really felt miserable. But fortunately, it revived and flew off again. I marched on, as miserable as ever.

Finally, over to my right, something very red caught my eye. It was red and round and glistening under some cool, green leaves on the shady side of the road. I saw another red thing, and then another. Then suddenly, I saw whole bunches of small, red, juicy round

65

things. Wild raspberries! They were everywhere. And boy, was I hungry! That was too much for me.

Apparently, no one had been down Arrowhead Trail for quite a few days. The berries had all ripened at once, rosy and sweet. And they were all mine! I pulled off my T-shirt and made a knapsack of it. Then I began shoveling raspberries into it. There were hundreds of them. First I just crammed them into my mouth. Then I waited till I had big cupfuls in my shirt and crammed those into my mouth. Then I just plain gave up being miserable, because the raspberries tasted too delicious and my stomach felt too good. After that, I guess I walked and picked raspberries for a couple of hours.

I was so busy, I didn't notice that the cotton ball clouds had blown in. When I finally stopped eating and looked up, they were black and almost covered the sky. I'd wandered quite a way down Arrowhead Trail. In fact, I was well onto the Ahlstroms' property. I'd wandered in the back way.

It's funny how, in the woods, you can hear the rain, hear it beating in the leaves, long before you feel it. Well, the minute I looked up, I heard the rain. I knew it was raining, but I didn't feel anything. Then, *splat, splat*. One by one, fat, heavy drops began drumming on my head. I was soaked in three minutes.

I was about fifty yards from the Ahlstroms' guesthouse. The guesthouse has a big garage where Maynard and Oscar kept the Chevy and their equipment: a lawn mower, a snowmobile, and a broken-down snowblower. They also had an ancient Victrola in the garage, which they used to let me crank up and play. They had boxes of inch-thick old records for it. My favorite was "Cloe." The garage door had been broken for years, so I decided to make a dash for it and sit out the storm inside.

It was late afternoon, but the sky was so black it seemed like night. I stumbled along through the woods in semi-darkness, in the direction of the guesthouse.

Suddenly, something caught me across the shins. It was sharp and cut my skin through my pants. I fell forward and found myself tangled in a wire fence. The top wire scraped the bridge of my nose.

There was a space where someone had already pushed up the bottom wire. I bent down, pushed up on the wires, and was crawling through the mud to the other side, when the sky lit up like the Fourth of July. A ball of light jumped out of the sky, rolled down the fence, and splashed against a tree. In a blaze of red on silver, I read the words KEEP OUT. It's all over, I thought. I've been zapped by an electric fence. God has finally punished me.

Then a clap and a clatter and a clang filled my ears, like a roll of fifty bass drums and fifty sets of cymbals. I wanted to run, but my shoes felt like someone had poured cement into them. Finally it dawned on me. The fireworks and cymbals were just an ordinary old lightning and thunderstorm at the lake. If anyone had clocked me for the fifty-yard dash into that guesthouse garage, I'd have broken a world record.

15

As I suspected, the garage door latch was still broken. I crept into a long, musty room. The smell of dust and mold was just as I remembered it. I was afraid to turn on a light. Then, gradually, my eyes got used to the gloom and I looked around. The Chevy was gone. But the snowmobile and rusty snowblower still sat in the corner where I remembered them. Not much use for that sort of thing in Arizona. The Victrola was gone. My heart sank a little. Cranking those scratchy voices out of the phonograph was like hearing Maynard and Oscar themselves. I wished they'd left it behind for me. Instead there was a stack of suitcases and cardboard boxes in its place. I crept over to the corner, hoping to find one old record left behind as a souvenir. "Cloe," maybe. Instead, I tripped over the corner of a suitcase. There was a loud crash and the tinkling of breaking glass as one of the boxes toppled, spilling its contents onto the cement floor.

Cards, binders, posters, pictures, scattered around me in confused piles. Then from out of the mess, a baseball rolled lazily toward me. It stopped a few inches from my hand. It was an old, used ball, stained with dirt and grass. But when I picked it up, I realized that it was also covered with a lot of smudged writing. I could barely make it out.

Giants 6, Dodgers 3

August 23, 1985

My heart skipped a beat. There was more. Slowly, I recognized it. The ball had been autographed by every member of the Giants team.

What a find! Dazed, I stared down at the boxes. Who knew what other treasures I might discover here?

I decided to pick up the stuff that I'd spilled. I know you're not supposed to snoop around in other people's things. Cleaning up, however, is different.

First, my hands found a long rectangular carton. I recognized the shape immediately, and started to shake. 1979 Topps. A complete set. I almost fainted. Next I flipped through a battered blue binder. It was filled with mint-condition cards — Mickey Mantle, Willie Mays, Hank Aaron, Bob Clemente, Don Drysdale. I found a Giants pennant, a Brewers cap, an old leather mitt. My head was swimming. I staggered backward and almost stepped on a broken picture frame. When I knelt down to look at it, I found myself staring face to face at the Yankee Clipper himself! He was in his Yankee pinstripes ready to bat. The photograph had a lot of writing on it. The penmanship was faded and hard to make out. But the last four words were so clear, you didn't need to read anything else: "Your friend, Joe DiMaggio." For the second time that day, I thought I'd died. Only this time, I'd gone to heaven.

But just as I was catching my breath, the door to the garage opened. The light switched on. I was face to face with someone else holding a bat. Only this time it wasn't a photograph. And it wasn't Joe DiMaggio. It was the mysterious man Dad and I had seen from the canoe.

He wore the same torn orange and black T-shirt he was wearing early that morning. He had the same angry sparks in his sad black eyes, and he was scowling behind a full black mustache and beard. My knees went weak, and my chest felt like someone had just knocked the wind out of me.

The man was holding the baseball bat in both hands. He held it high over his right shoulder, as if he was ready to hit a home run or something. Only, instead of a home run, he was ready to knock my block off.

"Who's there?" The man's narrowed eyes searched the room for the intruder.

I was still on my knees behind the overturned box. I was so scared that I knew if I tried to speak, no words would have come out of my mouth.

"I said, who's there?" The man's gruff voice filled the garage. "You'd better come out."

This time the man started walking toward my corner of the room. He was poking around with the baseball bat. In another second, he'd have been standing in front of me.

"I'm sorry. I'm so sorry." The words bubbled out of my lips as I stood up. "Please don't hit me. I just wanted to get out of the rain."

The jet black eyes looked down and met mine. Then

the strong, broad shoulders relaxed and a long, loud sigh escaped from the man's mouth. He dropped the bat, closed his eyes, and shook his head.

"A kid. Man, what's the matter with you? It's just a kid."

I looked around to see whom he was talking to. Then I realized, the man was talking to himself.

"Look, kid, it's stopped rainin'. Just get out of here, okay? I'm not goin' to give you any trouble, but just get out of here and go home."

He sounded weary, and his eyes lost all their anger and fear as he spoke. I wasn't afraid anymore, either. In fact, I realized there was something reassuring, almost familiar, about the man.

"So get goin'."

"Of course. Sure. Um, I'm really sorry. Honest."

"Yeah, well just don't go snoopin' around here anymore, understand?"

The uneasiness crept back into his voice.

It was crazy, I know, but once I realized that the guy wasn't going to hurt me, all I could think about was baseball — all that incredible stuff. Whoever had bought the Ahlstroms' property must be a major baseball fan — like me. I had to find out who it was. I had to find out why all these priceless treasures were piled in a cardboard box in a musty, dirty garage. If this man was the caretaker maybe he didn't realize how valuable they were. The least I could do was tell him. Whoever owned that box would surely be upset to find his collection stored in the garage. Then again, maybe this guy *was* the owner and didn't realize how

71

valuable the things were. Or maybe the owner was somebody's mother. Maybe the owner would sell the collection to me! I had to ask.

"Uh, who collected all the baseball stuff?" I was almost at the garage door when I blurted out the question.

"What?" The man's eyes narrowed again, giving his face the angry scowl I'd noticed before.

"Looks like somebody's a real baseball fan. You know, the cards and the autographed ball." I didn't mention the Joe DiMaggio picture. That was what I wanted most of all. "I collect baseball memorabilia, too."

But the man didn't answer. Instead, he looked scared again. He turned quickly away, and his voice became quiet and angry. "I told you to get out of here, kid. You forget what you saw in this garage. Do you hear? You don't mention anything about this to anyone. And don't ever come around here again, or you'll be sorry. I'll have the police here. Understand? I won't call them this time because I feel sorry for you. But if I see you in here again, I'll have you arrested for trespassin' and attempted burglary. Got that? Now go home and don't tell anyone you were here."

"I won't tell anyone. Really. I promise, I promise," I mumbled as I ran out the door.

"Trespassing. Attempted burglary." The words pounded in my ears all the way down Arrowhead Trail.

When I got to the cabin, my knees were still wobbling, and I guess I must have looked pale.

"Josh, where were you? We were ready to call the police. You're soaked. When the storm blew up and you didn't come home, we were scared to death."

My dad was hugging me.

"Are you okay? You look like you saw a ghost!"

I was still shaking.

"Yeah. I'm okay. I'm okay," I repeated. "Only don't call the police. Whatever you do, please don't call the police."

16

"We've got a surprise for you," my dad said.

I was sitting in front of the fire. He'd wrapped me up in his big robe. And Barbara had made me a mug of hot chocolate and a bowl of chili. I hated to admit it, but I loved Barbara's chili.

"A surprise?" I couldn't imagine what kind of surprise my dad could have in the middle of a lightning and thunderstorm. What's more, I had some surprises for him. I could tell him about the mysterious caretaker and about the autographed baseball and the picture of Joe DiMaggio. I had a *lot* of surprises for him. Then I remembered my promise. I was deciding whether to tell my father anyway, when Barbara walked into the living room holding my lost suitcase. For that second, she wasn't just smiling. She actually looked happy.

"Ta da!"

Then I forgot all about what happened in the Ahlstroms' garage. I plowed through the suitcase. All my treasures were there: my Giants hat, my Slug Smith mitt, my mint Willie Mays card, which was in better condition than the one in the garage, and my 1986 mint Topps set. I set the baseball card box in my lap and opened it. Then I started sorting out my cards.

I do this periodically. I sort the cards by team. Then sometimes I resort them by position. Or I resort the teams according to standing. Anyway, there I sat, in front of the fire, plugged into my headphones, listening to The Cure, and sorting my baseball cards. It was raining cats and dogs outside again, but I didn't care. I was happy.

I'd decided to pull out all the right fielders in the National League, and compare their batting averages with the averages of the third basemen. Right fielders are usually good hitters. Babe Ruth was a right fielder. So I pulled out Tony Gwynn from the Padres, and Mike Marshall from the Dodgers; Dave Parker from the Reds, and Darryl Strawberry from the Mets. Then I pulled out Slug Smith from the Giants. Actually, I didn't have to pull Slug's card. I'd memorized his statistics long ago. But I pulled the card anyway, for the sake of completeness, and set it on the coffee table with the picture facing me.

Slug was standing, holding his bat. He wore the Giants white home uniform. He held his bat high over his right shoulder, ready to hit a home run. Suddenly something clicked. I picked up the card, blinked, and looked at it again. The batting position — it reminded me of something.

Slug's eyes were narrowed. He was really concentrating on that ball. His eyes were black, and kind of sad, and kind of angry. Then it dawned on me. The eyes — I'd seen those eyes. Seen them that very afternoon staring at me in the Ahlstroms' garage. In the garage, the rest of the face was covered by a thick bushy beard. But the eyes and the stance were unmistakable. Of course! That explained everything! The man in the garage was Slug Smith!

I was so excited I almost tipped over my hot chocolate and spilled it on my baseball cards. Boy, would that have been a disaster! My dad was in the basement getting firewood. I started to run downstairs to tell him about Slug Smith. But suddenly I remembered —

"You forget what you saw in this garage. Do you hear? You don't mention anything about this to anyone."

"I won't tell anyone. Really. I promise, I promise."

I sat back down in the chair by the fire. For a month, reporters and sports fans had been trying to find out what happened to Slug Smith. His teammates didn't know. His manager didn't know. His secretary didn't know. Even his agent didn't know. The whereabouts of Slug Smith was a deep, dark secret. And for some reason or another, Slug Smith wanted it kept that way. I was probably the only person in the world who knew where Slug Smith was. But I'd promised him I wouldn't tell anyone.

My dad walked back upstairs with the firewood. He started piling it in the bin next to my chair. I was so excited, I thought I'd burst. But I just kept on sorting my baseball cards. I didn't say a word about the secret I knew. After all, I'd made a promise. And a promise to Slug Smith was sacred.

17

A few days after I met Slug Smith in the garage, Dad and I planned a morning canoe trip to God's Country.

God's Country is one of my favorite places. Besides being a bait shop and soda fountain rolled into one, it has the best candy counter I've ever seen. I mean, God's Country has every kind of candy bar ever invented, including brands you rarely see in the city. Like Neccos, or the long Tootsie Rolls. I didn't even think they made them anymore. And God's Country also has every kind of gum you can imagine. Gum shaped like little hamburgers, gum in tobacco pouches, pizza gum, even garbage-shaped gum in tiny garbage cans. But the thing I like best at God's Country is the little wax soda bottles in miniature cartons. You bite off the wax bottle tops and drink the soda. Those are cool! I mean who would expect a little bait and tackle shop in the middle of nowhere to have such great candy?

Actually, I have a theory about that. I think that many years ago, Ethel Nordquist, the owner, bought up cases and cases of candy. All summer she sold it. All winter she ate it.

Mrs. Nordquist is the fattest lady I've ever seen. I honestly believe she could be in the *Guinness Book of World Records*. She's that huge! Each upper arm is the size of a watermelon. Her head looks like a pimple. She's at least four feet wide. When she stands behind the soda fountain, she can serve the whole counter without moving. And that's a good thing, because she moves very, very slowly.

Well, that morning I was sitting at the soda fountain drinking my root beer float, staring at Mrs. Nordquist's arms, and imagining where she buys clothes, when, who should come in, but Slug Smith! Dad was picking suckers out of the bait tank. Slug walked right by him, and Dad didn't even notice!

I knew that telling Dad about Slug Smith was breaking my promise. But I was going crazy keeping it a secret. So I decided that giving Dad a hint about Slug was different from telling him. Right? It wasn't my fault if Dad guessed who his neighbor was.

"Take me out to the ball game. Take me out to the crowd," I sang while I helped Dad scoop suckers. Dad pretended he didn't hear me. Maybe I was singing too softly. I tried a little louder.

"So it's one, two, three strikes you're —" My own dad stuck a quarter in the juke box to drown me out. I felt dumb, but I didn't give up.

Mrs. Nordquist had finally made it to the other side of the store where Slug was looking at lures.

"Lars Youngdahl caught a sixteen-pound Northern

78

with this here Dardevle. It was just last month, over on Little Sandy."

Mrs. Nordquist knows who caught every fish within twenty miles of Turtle Lake. For the last forty years! She even knows what lure they used. That's almost as incredible as how fat she is.

"Got any Big League Chew, Mrs. Nordquist?" I interrupted in a loud voice. Then I called to my dad who was at the cash register. "Hey, Dad, is it okay if I buy some Big League Chew? Get it? Big League Chew? Gum in a tobacco —"

"Josh, stop yelling." Dad looked really embarrassed. I turned around to see if Slug had noticed me yet. I guess he had. He was gone.

I didn't catch one glimpse of Slug for three days after that. For two days, I watched his front door through the trees from our beach. No sign of him. And was I sunburned! I began to worry that Slug had moved. Or died. I had to find out what happened to him. Finally I thought up a plan. *I'd* promised never to set foot on his property again. Wendy hadn't.

But I needed Wendy's help. Wendy and I had ignored each other since our fight the morning after we arrived. I knew she didn't like me, but I also knew she was bored. It would have been hard not to know! Wendy told Barbara she was bored about ten times a day.

"Want to play some baseball with me?" I'd finally found Wendy sitting in a little thicket of bushes overlooking the beach. I was kind of surprised to see her there. That thicket used to be my hide-out when I was little. I used to sit in there for hours and pretend I was a spy.

"You play baseball?" What else would you expect Wendy to say?

"Sure I do, Wendy. Come on. It'll be fun. I'll teach you."

Wendy cracked up. For some reason, she thought that was really funny. But she followed me to get a ball and my bat.

My plan was that Wendy would pitch the ball to me, and I'd slam it over the fence onto Slug's property. I'd send Wendy over to get it. Of course, Slug would want to know who the great batter was.

"If it lands over the fence, just climb under the wire and get it. The only thing is that you should ring the bell and tell the guy who lives there who you are and what you're doing."

"No way! Your dad says that guy's weird."

"No. No. He's really okay. Honest. I've met him. He's a great guy." That wasn't exactly a lie. He is "great." It's just a different kind of "great."

Wendy shook her head. "I don't know." Then she laughed. "What am I worried about? You'll never hit the ball over the fence."

I would have, if Wendy'd pitched the ball half decently. It's amazing how lucky girls can be in sports. I could swear she was throwing curve balls at me.

"Okay, Josh," she said finally. "My turn to bat."

"No way!" I wasn't going to waste my time pitching to her. At that rate, we'd never find out if Slug was home.

"Come on, Josh. Just once. This is getting really boring." See what I mean?

So I tossed her one ball. I have to admit, I tried to make it easy so it wouldn't be too embarrassing for her. Well, the next thing I knew, the ball was sailing over the fence and through the trees. The next thing after that, I heard a crash! I ran to the corner of the beach where I could see Slug's house. You got it. Wendy had broken Slug Smith's front window.

We did find out that Slug was home. The way he was hollering when he ran out the door, I kind of wished he *had* moved.

"All right. Who did that? Come on!"

Not me! I'd run to my hide-out in the bushes. I could see everything perfectly. Slug was chasing Wendy up the beach. She still had the bat in her hand.

"You hit that ball through my window, kid!" For a second I thought maybe Wendy would try to blame it on me. Slug definitely wasn't impressed with the batting.

"Look, sir, I'm really sorry. Honest. I didn't mean —"

"Listen, kid. I already told your brother once to stay off my property or I'd call the police. That goes for you and your baseballs, too. Do you hear?"

"Just let me get my mom. We'll pay for the window."

That was when I saw Slug panic. "Your mother!" He looked over his shoulder as if there were someone behind him. "Get her mother? That's all I need! Look, kid. Get it straight. I don't want to see you, or your nosy brother, or your cousin, or your uncle, or your mother. Just leave me alone." Was he angry! He climbed under the fence and stomped back to his house.

"What about the ball?!" I couldn't believe Wendy yelled that. Next thing, my baseball came sailing over the trees. It landed about an inch from my head.

" 'Don't worry, the caretaker's a really great guy.' " Wendy was peering into the thicket at me. "You planned that just to get me into trouble, didn't you? And I thought you were actually trying to be friendly. Well, I know better now, Josh Morris." Wendy ran back to the house, crying.

18

After Wendy broke Slug Smith's window, she stopped talking to me altogether. As if it were my fault! In fact, after Wendy broke Slug's window, Wendy and I never saw each other. It was Barbara's idea. Barbara called it a "time out."

I have to give Barbara credit for finally realizing that Wendy and I had absolutely nothing in common. I frankly began to worry that Dad and Barbara didn't have much in common, either. In fact, I even started to feel sorry for Barbara; during "time out," Barbara never saw my dad. And I'd have felt sorry for anybody who had to spend all her time with Wendy.

Dad and I woke up early in the morning and went fishing. In the afternoon, we went swimming. Wendy practiced her ballet in the morning. In the afternoon, she and Barbara played tennis at Camp Tecumseh. The only time all four of us got together was at dinner. That was just fine with me!

At dinner, the only people who talked were Barbara and Dad. Occasionally, I talked to Barbara. Just the basics. And I always remembered to be polite. I got a lot of brownie points that way. Wendy was almost never polite.

"The pie is delicious." Barbara loved compliments on her cooking, so I started throwing one in every night. And I didn't mention that I prefer apple pie the way my mother makes it, with the apples cut in slices instead of "chips." And I didn't mention that my mom's pie crust tasted better than Barbara's. Grownups hate comparisons like that. Especially when the comparison is with a relative.

"Well, thank you, Josh. It's such a pleasure to hear you say that." Barbara looked over at my dad. They smiled at each other.

"Your mom certainly is a good cook, isn't she, Wendy?" Dad thought he'd finally found a topic Wendy and I agreed on.

"Grandma's a better cook. Her crust is thinner." Wendy had picked every bit of apple out of her piece of pie and left the crust smeared over her plate. It looked disgusting.

Dad whispered to Barbara, "I thought your mother was dead."

"Her other grandmother," Barbara whispered back. Barbara and my dad did a lot of whispering that summer. "You know, Sid's mother."

"Ohhh."

I jumped up to clear the table. People like my dad don't give up easily, though.

"How about if tomorrow we pack a picnic and all sail to Goose Island?"

Goose Island is across the lake from Arrowhead

Point. With a good wind, you can sail there in fifteen minutes.

"That's a great idea, Ted." That was Barbara, of course. "But maybe we should postpone it. You know, till after the . . ."

"Forget the time out!" my dad exclaimed. "Let's all have a party."

"A party?" I looked over my shoulder from the sink where I was piling dishes. At the table sat two smiling grown-ups and one very unhappy kid. It wasn't promising. "But there's nothing to celebrate."

"Of course there is." My dad beamed. He sounded just like Mr. Brady on TV. But nothing was going to turn Wendy and me into the Brady Bunch. "Of course we have something to celebrate. Our new family."

Wendy got up from the table and belly flopped onto the living room couch. "Well, barf me out the door!"

Actually, the "family picnic" started out pretty well. The weather was great — really hot and still. Just the way I like it. Barbara made leftover roast beef sandwiches with homemade bread. There were celery sticks, carrots, and olives. Dad made lemonade for the cooler. And for dessert, Barbara made chocolate cream pie. Even I was looking forward to it.

We filled the cooler, piled the food into the picnic basket, and packed our bathing suits and towels. Then we all boarded the sailboat.

The sailboat is not very big, but we figured four of us could just fit. Wendy and Barbara sat in the pit. I manned the tiller, and Dad sailed. Wendy held the picnic basket on her lap. Barbara carried the cooler.

We no sooner cast off than a breeze filled our sail. In two tacks we were halfway to Goose Island. I know my dad's not the world's best sailor, but so far, no one else could have guessed.

Then, just as suddenly as the breeze came up, it died. It happens like that on the lake. It happens to me all the time. Hard as Dad tried, he couldn't pick up the tiniest puff of wind. Motor boats with water skiers whizzed by. We stood still.

"Darndest thing!" Dad muttered. Wendy and Barbara stared at him. I think they expected him to blow the boat to Goose Island. "There's not a puff of wind."

We drifted awhile. Dad and Barbara admired the shoreline and picked out lots where their friends were building cabins. Wendy dangled her long, knobby legs over the side of the boat.

"Watch out," I whispered to Wendy. "A ten-foot muskie could bite off your toe. Happened last summer on Little Sandy." Wendy didn't fall for it.

Fifteen minutes later, nothing had happened.

"Darndest thing!" When my dad gets nervous and there are kids around, he repeats "darndest thing" about a million times. So I could tell he was desperate. To make it worse, a Sailfish just a few hundred yards away was moving swiftly to shore.

"How come the other sailboat works?" There was

only one thing I admired about Wendy. She always asked the question I wouldn't dare ask.

Dad ignored her. He was pulling the sail back and forth across the boat, searching for a breeze. It was no use.

"Mom, look at that sailboat docking. It made it across the lake just fine."

"Yes, I see it, dear," Barbara whispered. "Now just be quiet and let Ted concentrate."

But all the concentration in the world wasn't going to move our boat.

After another fifteen minutes, everyone was restless.

"Darndest thing!"

"Are you sure you know how to sail this boat?"

"Wendy, you're being —" Barbara started to warn.

"Of course I know how to sail," Dad snapped. "I've been sailing on this lake since I was younger than you, little lady." I thought Dad was going to bite Wendy's head off. About time, too. But all Dad did was start Wendy crying and get Barbara mad.

I tried to change the subject. "Boy, am I hungry. Since we're not going anywhere, we might as well eat that delicious lunch you made, Barbara." My stomach was growling.

Wendy stood up to shove me the picnic basket. "Here. All you think about is your stomach."

"Ah, Wendy, I don't think you should —"

Dad tried to warn her, but it was too late. Just as I was reaching for the basket, a gust of wind rose out of nowhere. The boom spun around. I ducked in time. Wendy wasn't so lucky. The boom struck her shoulder, knocking her clear off the boat and into the water. The terrible part was, our picnic basket flew overboard with her.

"Our lunch! Wendy, get the basket!" I stood on the bow shouting. Wendy was bobbing up and down in the water.

"Wendy! Darling! Are you hurt?" Barbara screamed and dived in after Wendy. She didn't need to. Much as I hate to admit this, Wendy probably is an even better swimmer than I am.

"Somebody save the picnic basket!" But just as I yelled, another gust of wind spun the sail, and the boat tipped over. As I thrashed around in the water, I saw the picnic basket disappear below the surface. A few seconds later, two pieces of celery floated up alongside me. That was the only part of that lunch that was ever seen again.

19

While Barbara and Wendy treaded water, Dad and I tried to right the boat. We weren't having much luck, either. Then, out of nowhere, we heard a voice.

"Need some help?"

I looked up, and saw Slug Smith sitting in a little motor boat watching us. Dad and I were so busy, we hadn't heard him approach.

"Can I help you with that?" he repeated. "I brought a rope. I saw you tip over from my dock. Here."

Slug threw Dad one end of the rope. In a few minutes, they had the boat right-side up in the water.

"Thanks very much. I owe you one." Dad and Barbara were back in the sailboat. "By the way, I think we're neighbors. My name's Ted Morris. Come over and have a drink with us later."

Slug was wearing a baseball cap. He tugged the visor down low over his eyes. "Some other time, man."

Then Wendy started sobbing.

"I'm not going in the same boat with Josh." Wendy was a good swimmer, but not good enough to swim to shore.

"Wendy, please . . ." Barbara sounded weary.

"Yeah," I blurted out. "Give your mom a break."

Barbara looked at me, surprised. All Wendy did was get more hysterical.

"I almost drown and all that creep cares about is lunch. I'm not sitting next to him in that boat. I hate him."

Slug turned around to see what the problem was. Then Barbara said something I'll never forget. "Sir. Sir, excuse me." She was calling to the man in the boat. To Slug Smith. "Sorry to bother you. We've got a problem. Could you give Josh here a ride to the dock?"

Slug looked me over suspiciously. Then he swung his boat around beside me.

"Why did I get myself mixed up in this?" he muttered to an invisible friend. "Get in, kid."

I could have actually kissed my stepmother. I scrambled over the side of the motorboat. Next thing I knew, I was seated beside the National League leader for most RBIs in 1984.

"Hey, man, you're gettin' me all wet!"

I looked down, and realized we were sitting in a puddle of water. The water was running off of my wet clothes.

"Sit over there, will ya?"

I stood up, tripped over a fishnet, and almost capsized the boat.

"Watch out! Can't you look where you're goin', for cryin' out loud?" Slug rolled his eyes. Then, once again, he addressed his imaginary companion. "Darn kid's nothin' but trouble, I swear . . ."

"I'm sorry, Slug. Honest, I don't mean to cause you trouble."

"That's okay, man," Slug replied absently. "Sorry I snapped at you."

We sat in silence for a minute. Then Slug's eyes narrowed. He stared at me.

"What'd you just call me?"

"Nothing. I didn't call you anything." I was so flustered, I didn't realize I'd given myself away.

Slug shook his head impatiently.

"Just now, you called me *somethin'*. What'd you say?"

"I didn't say anything. Honest."

Slug pulled down his cap and looked over his shoulder. But I could tell he didn't believe me.

We were just a few yards from the dock when Slug turned to me again.

"You know who I am, don't you?"

"Yeah."

"Does your family know? Your mom and dad and your sister?"

"No."

I wanted to correct the part about my "mom" and my "sister," but it seemed like the wrong time.

"How'd you recognize me?"

I didn't know what to say. It was kind of a long answer. I mean, including coming from San Francisco, losing my suitcase, sorting my baseball cards and everything. We were almost at the dock.

"I guess because you're my hero." In a way, that said it all.

We'd reached our dock. The sailboat was still far away. Slug turned off the motor and paddled his boat up to the landing. Then he caught the dock post with his fishing net to bring the boat alongside. I stepped off.

"Thanks," I mumbled. My heart felt like it was climbing into my throat. My dream had come true — I'd had ten minutes alone with Slug Smith — and I'd blown it! I dripped water all over him, nearly capsized his boat, and then called him "my hero" like some goofy girl in the movies. Now I'd never see him again.

"Hey, kid." I was halfway up the dock when I heard his voice. "You said you're a baseball fan. Do you play baseball, too?"

I swung around. "I sure do." My heart was back in my chest, only now it was thumping so loud I could hear it. "I'm on a team and everything. I'm a right fielder, just like you."

"Well, what d'ya know." He stopped talking and seemed to be thinking about something. "See, my arm's gettin' a little stiff. Maybe you could stop by sometime, and I'll toss you a few."

I actually got dizzy when he said that. And my mouth got dry and the words stuck in my throat like peanut butter.

"Sure," I squeaked.

"But don't get nosy, understand? Just throw the ball."

"Of course."

"And don't tell anybody."

I shook my head.

As he started up the motor, he called above the noise. "See you tomorrow, kid."

"Okay."

Then Slug Smith waved and roared off around the point.

20

"By the way, what'd you make of that fellow yesterday? The guy you rode home with."

Dad and I were having breakfast. Of course, I hadn't mentioned a word about the ride.

"Nothing."

"He seemed a little odd to me. Secretive. Like he didn't want anyone to see him."

"Seemed okay to me."

"Did he say anything? Did he tell you his name?"

"Nope. He didn't say a thing."

"Hmm."

I got up and cleared the table. Clearing the table's a good thing to do when you don't want to discuss something. Your parents are so glad you're helping, they don't interrupt you.

"Well . . . good of him to rescue us . . ." my dad trailed off. "How about a trip to God's Country today? We'll need more bait." Dad opened the refrigerator.

Dad and I always keep our night crawlers in the

refrigerator. It's the only place where they stay fresh. But that morning, the bait shelf was empty.

The day before, after the boat trip, everyone arrived home hungry. Wendy ran into the kitchen looking for the leftover potato salad. Barbara makes great potato salad. She puts big slices of hard boiled egg in it and lots of pickles and celery. I'd remembered the potato salad, too. In fact, I'd just finished eating all of it. So I was standing there in the kitchen when Wendy opened the door.

She took out the carton of night crawlers, thinking it was the potato salad. She was so hungry she didn't even bother to get a plate. She just grabbed a spoon, tore off the carton top, and dug into a fresh serving of fat, juicy worms. The spoon was halfway to her mouth when she noticed. Then she dropped the carton and screamed. Dad heard her all the way down at the dock.

I started laughing so hard I couldn't stand up. I had to lie down on the kitchen floor. Then, do you know what Wendy did? She walked over to me (I was laughing so hard, I was crying by that time) and she kicked me. In the leg. I couldn't believe it! I'd never been kicked by a girl before. And you know what? It really hurt. Then Wendy ran upstairs and locked her door.

Barbara rushed in next. She was really mad. She said worms did not belong in the refrigerator. Then she made *me* clean up the mess and throw it all in the garbage.

"Better get minnows this time." Dad had closed the refrigerator. He was sitting at the table making a list of things to buy at God's Country. "We can hang them off the dock in a bucket. And you can buy that Dardevle you wanted."

Dad knew I wanted a Dardevle lure. He was trying to make up for Barbara getting mad at me. *He* was the one who put the worms in the refrigerator!

"Would you mind if I didn't come, Dad? I've got a lot of . . . ah . . . reading to do."

"Reading?" Dad was shocked.

"Book reports for school."

"But you're not going to that school next year."

He had a point. "Well . . . they're really strict in San Francisco. I'm mailing in the reports."

Dad wasn't buying it. "Sounds like a very difficult school out there . . ."

"Honest, I'm supposed to mail in the book reports. Otherwise they won't promote me."

Dad shook his head. "I'll let you play a video game at God's Country."

"No. No, that's okay. You see, I've got a little headache."

Now I know that when you're making up excuses, you should always stick to one. Changing excuses is a dead giveaway.

"Josh, just what is it you're planning to do today?"

"Read. I'm going to read."

"All right. But you'd better not be planning any mischief, young man."

"Oh, no."

Dad eyed me suspiciously. "Just to be on the safe side, I want a report myself, on the book you're reading. We'll talk about it tonight, Josh."

That was all I needed! You know, parents are pretty smart after all.

21

As soon as Dad left for God's Country, I took off down Arrowhead Trail. I noticed a few patches of raspberries, but I didn't stop to pick them. I crawled under the wire fence and ran until I reached the garage. There, I stopped for a minute to catch my breath. Then I walked to the main house and knocked on the door. I waited. No answer. I knocked again. Waited some more. Still no answer. Then I banged on the door. Nobody came. Finally I walked around the house and peered in the windows. The place was a mess, but there was no one inside.

I sat down on the front porch, feeling miserable. It didn't make any sense. Slug had told me to meet him. Then a thought struck me so hard, it hurt. Maybe I'd just dreamed the part where Slug asked me to play baseball with him. Maybe none of yesterday afternoon really happened. Maybe I just wanted it so much, I'd convinced myself it did happen. I was so disappointed, I started to cry.

"What took you so long?" The sound of a voice startled me. Slug stood in the clearing, holding a fishing rod. "I've been waitin' all mornin' for you." He sounded sort of mad.

"I'm sorry." Boy, did I feel stupid. "I'd have come earlier, but I had to make sure my dad didn't see me."

Now Slug sounded even madder. "Your dad? He doesn't know who I am, does he?"

"No, no. That's the whole point. My dad thinks you're kind of weird." The minute I said it, I knew it had come out wrong.

Slug glanced over his shoulder. "Can you beat that! He thinks *I'm* weird." He shook his head. "You know, I've been thinkin' *you* people were the weird ones. I've never heard so much noise as since you all moved in. Every day, music blarin', and people screamin' and shriekin'. You're one kooky family all right."

That made me laugh. I thought of Wendy's night-crawler potato salad.

"That's just Wendy."

"Your sister?"

"*Not* my sister," I shot back. "She's my . . . my . . ." The word stuck in my throat. "Stepsister." I spit it out.

Slug nodded. "I can dig it. And the lady's your stepmother."

I nodded.

"Let's get us a baseball." Slug was already running toward the garage. There he dug bats, mitts, and two baseballs out of the cardboard box.

When I picked up one of the balls, I saw that it was autographed. "Hey, we can't use this. It's valuable."

"Valuable?" Slug replied, surveying the contents of the baseball box I'd tipped over. "This stuff is junk."

"Junk!" I hollered. "It's priceless!"

Slug didn't answer, but a sad smile crept over his face.

"If it was junk, you wouldn't have brought it," I insisted.

"You're right, kid." Slug spoke softly. "It ain't junk. It's important stuff. Important to us, anyway. Important," he repeated to himself, "for remembering." As we walked outside, Slug carefully hung the broken picture of Joe DiMaggio on a peg by the garage door.

We stood in the clearing between the main house and the guesthouse, tossing the ball.

"Yeeow!" Slug's first toss was like a rocket. I tried to duck out of its path. Too late. It clipped me on the elbow.

"Hey, kid. You okay? I thought you said you were a baseball player."

That remark hurt a thousand times more than the baseball.

"'Course I'm okay." My elbow was killing me. I blinked hard. "Wasn't ready."

I found the ball in the bushes and tossed it back. After that, Slug just threw underhand lobs. I could see what he thought of me! And to make matters worse, I kept dropping the ball. I was too busy trying to think of something to say.

Have you ever noticed how the longer you're with someone without talking, the harder it gets to talk? If you start out talking, you can say any stupid thing:

"Great weather we're having" or "Don't you love the way the air smells here?" or "How was the ride coming up?" But after staring at someone for ten minutes, it's impossible!

And let's face it, there were a million questions I was dying to ask Slug Smith. Most of them were "off limits." No questions about why he quit baseball. But the other questions were about baseball: "What was it like to hit the grand slam that sank the Dodgers' pennant bid in 1985?" or "What's Will Clark really like?" or "When you hit a home run, do you feel it in your bones when you walk up to bat?"

But nothing sounded right. So I stood there, dropping the ball, trying like crazy to think of something to say.

"I been wonderin'." At last! It was Slug who broke the silence.

I waited.

"What's a kid from Wisconsin doin' with me for a hero?"

Now that seemed like a stupider question than the ones I was thinking. Slug Smith is one of the greatest hitters of all time. Really. His name's a household word. Even my mother knows who he is. He could be anyone's hero.

"I'm not from Wisconsin. I'm from San Francisco."

"Hmm. You come here with your family for the summer?"

"Yeah. Every year I visit for six —" Then I stopped. This year, I wasn't just "visiting." This year, I was — my mind tried to change the subject. It changed the subject every night in bed when I thought about my mom, my house in San Francisco, Wilson School, stopping at the Guidis' every morning to pick up Danny. Every night, my mind changed the subject, just as I started to remember all those things.

"Every year, I visit for six weeks, but this year I'm . . . I'm . . ." Suddenly, my mind wouldn't change the subject anymore. "Staying."

Slug rolled his eyes. He caught the ball I'd tossed, and rubbed it in his glove. "You sure don't sound too happy about it, kid."

He meant to be nice, I think. But I was getting choked up, so I changed the subject.

"Well, you could be anyone's hero, Slug. You're even a TV star. Every kid in the country saw you broadcast the World Series with Howard Co —"

Suddenly the ball was screaming toward me. I ducked and then I froze.

"Say, you know what your problem is, kid?" I heard Slug laugh. "You're afraid of the baseball!"

22

That first training session with Slug was not what you'd call successful. My elbow was killing me! So I wasn't exactly disappointed when Slug sent me home.

"Come early tomorrow! Y'hear?"

"Sure!" I couldn't believe my ears. I was being invited back!

"And bring your own glove. Mine's too big."

"Holy cow! You bet."

My elbow ached all the way home, but in a way it felt good. After all, I hurt it playing ball with Slug Smith!

When I ran up the steps to the porch of our cabin, you'd have thought everybody had spent the afternoon waiting for me.

"So where've you been all day? Did you finally find a rock big enough to crawl under?"

I don't have to tell you who said that. Wendy was curled up on the porch swing. Barbara sat beside her.

Our porch swing is big. A three-seater. And it's covered with plastic cushions. The cushions are blue with big rainbows splashed all over them. The rainbows are one of the first things I can remember from when I was a baby. Mom and I used to sit on those

cushions for hours and swing. I'd stare at the rainbows. Even before I knew what rainbows were.

Now every time I went out on the porch, Wendy
was sitting on the swing. That pretty much meant I
couldn't use it anymore.

"Please excuse Wendy's rude comments, Josh."
Barbara sounded really embarrassed. "What Wendy
means is, we were starting to worry about you."

I think that was the first time I took a good look
at my two new relatives. Usually, I tried to pretend
they weren't there. But that afternoon, I started to
notice things. Barbara has straight, brown hair and a
long face with a pointed nose. My friend Danny would
say she looks like a friendly collie. Wendy has lots of
curly, black hair. That afternoon, it wasn't in a doughnut. Wendy looks a lot more acceptable without the
doughnut. She has blue eyes and black eyelashes that
make an outline around each eye. Wendy's face is
round. Danny would probably call her a Lhasa apso.
What I mean is, for the first time, I noticed that Wendy
and Barbara looked like they might be nice.

"Where've you been, son?" That was Dad.

I don't think I've gotten that much attention since
the morning I walked to school in my pajama bot-
toms.

"Did you get a lot of reading done?" Dad stared
at the baseball I was holding.

"Sure did. I'll tell you all about it after dinner." I
raced upstairs and speed-read the first five chapters of
Kidnapped.

The next morning, getting out of the house was

even harder than getting in the evening before. I had to bring my glove. When I got downstairs for breakfast, Dad was waiting for me as usual.

"Let's go swimming. It's boiling already."

"No thanks, Dad. I don't feel like swimming today. I've got a headache."

"Hmm." Then Dad noticed the glove. "Looking for someone to play ball with?"

"No . . . no."

Dad looked at the glove again.

"I mean yes . . . well . . . not exactly."

"What exactly *do* you mean?"

"I was just . . . um . . . I was just looking at it." I tucked the glove under my arm. "I was just going to take a walk."

"I'd love to take a walk. Mind if I join you?"

"No . . . I mean yes. Yes, I mind." I cringed as I said it. "Dad, I'd just like to take a walk alone."

"Okay." My dad looked really unhappy. Barbara had already left for town to shop. I felt sorry for him.

"I'll find a quiet place and do a little reading, you know?" I picked up *Kidnapped* from the coffee table.

"Well, okay." Dad turned to go back into the kitchen. "Guess I didn't realize you'd turned into such a reader."

As I sped out the front door, I saw Wendy. She'd been watching me the whole time.

When I got to the Ahlstroms', Slug was sitting on the front steps waiting for me. He didn't look very happy to see me. And he didn't even bother to say good morning. Instead, he just asked a lot of questions.

"Listen, kid. The other day, you told me you play on a baseball team. Just which team is that?"

"My school team. Wilson Elementary. My old school in San Francisco." When I thought about my school, I felt a little lump form in my throat again.

"Have you got a coach there?"

I must not have looked like I'd had much coaching. "Of course we do."

"Well, when the ball's coming at you, you're supposed to try to catch it."

"I know . . ."

Slug threw up his hands and glanced over his shoulder. It was as if he was always talking to a little ghost, who followed him around. "He knows!" He looked back at me. "So why'd you duck?"

"I thought the ball was going to hit me."

Slug looked really disgusted. He was quiet for a long time. For a minute, I thought he was going to send me home again.

"You really want to play right field, kid?"

I nodded.

Slug walked to the center of the clearing. "Well then, you'd better learn a thing or two." Slug bent over and picked up a bat. "When the other team is up at bat, what are you supposed to be doin'?"

"Making outs."

"Right. And to make outs, what do you have to do?"

"Catch the ball."

"Right." Slug bent over again and picked up a baseball. "But you can't catch the ball if you duck."

"I know that."

"Well, you sure don't act like you know it." Slug shifted his weight from side to side and tapped his shoes with the bat. "See, when you're standin' out there in right field, you gotta want that ball. You gotta want it like it was a million-dollar bill floatin' in the breeze. There's no maybe, or let the infielder get it. You want that ball so bad, you can taste it. You don't wait around for the ball to bean you, boy. You *go after* it."

Slug tossed the ball in the air, brought his bat back over his right shoulder, and hammered a line drive through the trees. The ball hit the corner of the garage, taking off a shingle.

"See," I said. "That ball could knock all my teeth out." There was clearly plenty to be afraid of.

"Sure, kid. And you could trip and knock all your teeth out, too."

"But I make sure I don't. I'm careful."

"Listen to that!" Slug's little ghost must have been standing on a tree branch. "*Now* he's gettin' it!" He turned to face me. "And I make sure I don't get beaned by the ball. I catch it. Carefully."

"Huh?"

"That's right, kid. You gotta learn the steps. With a few lessons from Slug, it'll seem like catchin' butterflies."

That afternoon, Slug sent a zillion balls whizzing through the trees.

"Back up. Get behind it. Get your glove up early. *Prepare*. Don't stand out there daydreamin'."

"But I get bored. There's nothing to do in right field."

"Bored!" Slug threw up his hands. Now his little ghost was on third base. "Course you get bored. Anybody'd get bored just standin' there. You gotta think up stuff to do. Watch each batter. Take mental notes. Figure out how he hits. Figure out where he hits. There's plenty to do out there besides daydream, boy!"

"Well, I guess —"

"That's the whole point," Slug interrupted. "You *never* guess." He was warmed up now. "The second you see where the ball's headin', you start movin'. Get under it. Get that glove up. If the sun's in your eyes, use your glove to block out the sun. Then wait. That's what I mean by preparation. Give yourself plenty of time. Then just slow everything down."

"What?"

"Slow everything down. Like you were pullin' the switch on a movie projector. Put the whole game in slow motion. Breathe slower. Think slower. You can actually slow the ball down. Watch it move. Then say to yourself, 'Man, here comes the ball. I've got plenty of time, and I know where it's headin'.' After that, the ball will seem to be waitin' for you. You'll pluck it out of the sky, like a flutterin' butterfly."

"Wow!"

"Think you can do it?"

"I don't know, but that was beautiful!"

"What was beautiful?"

"The way you said that."

"The way I said it?" Slug looked angry. "Don't jive me, man. I talk like I got two left feet."

Then Slug whacked a ball at me. I backed up and held out my glove. Then I slowed everything down just as Slug said. The ball didn't exactly seem like a butterfly. It was more like a torpedo. But when I reached for it, I felt I had more time, and knew where it was heading.

I guess I really didn't know, because I missed the catch. But I wasn't afraid. For the first time, I wasn't afraid one bit.

23

However, walking home that night, I found something else to be afraid of. Crackling noises in the dark woods along the trail. They gave me a creepy feeling. Somehow I knew it wasn't a bird, or a frog, or a deer. I shivered and broke into a run for the cabin.

The next morning, along Arrowhead Trail, right where I heard the creepy noises, I found an empty banana Bubblicious wrapper. There was no way I could have dropped it. I hate banana Bubblicious. And it wasn't dropped by any deer. I shivered again.

"Okay, kid, remember what I said about slowing everything down when you're in right field?"

It was our third day of training. I'd brought over my bat (You should have seen me trying to explain that to my dad in the morning. I told him I needed it for a walking stick.), and we were having our first batting practice.

"Yeah. Sure." Slug's advice about slowing things down worked pretty well.

"You do the same thing when you bat."

Slug picked up a big bat. First he tapped his right Nike with the tip of the bat. Then he tapped his left. It was funny to see him do this even when he wasn't wearing his cleats; there was nothing to tap the dirt out of but I guess these things get to be a habit. Next he placed his feet about a yard apart and kind of wiggled his rear end, shifting from left to right. Then he shrugged his shoulders a few times, grasping both ends of the bat. I'd seen him do this a million times — every time he came to bat. In fact, I'd sort of memorized it. Finally he was ready.

"Okay, toss me one."

I lobbed him the ball. Then I watched. He looked relaxed, almost in slow motion as he took his bat back and waited. Then he swung. Not just the bat. It seemed like he swung his whole body at the ball. *Crack!* It wasn't a very good pitch either. Slug sent it sailing over the trees. It was my turn next. I tapped each of my turf shoes, planted my feet about a yard apart, wiggled my behind, and shrugged my shoulders.

"Ready," I yelled. But by that time, Slug was rolling on the ground laughing.

"What in tarnation was that all about, boy?"

"All what?"

"All that dancin' you just did."

"Dancing?"

"This here is called baseball, not the boogie."

Most kids would cry over a lot less. I blinked a few times and swallowed hard.

"I was just doing what you do."

That made Slug laugh even harder. He looked over his shoulder. "That's what I been doin'? No wonder my average is slippin'. Now listen here, boy. First, you tap your shoes to get the dirt out of your cleats."

"I know that."

"But, see, you ain't wearin' cleats."

"I know that, too." I decided it wasn't worth mentioning that he wasn't wearing them either.

"Next." I could tell this was going to be a long explanation. "You got your feet too far apart. I'm six foot three. I got my feet about a yard apart. How tall are you?"

"Four foot ten."

"You spread your feet a yard and you're doin' the splits. See what I mean?"

"Okay, okay."

"Next, you shift your weight from side to side, you know, to get your balance. It's kind of like usin' one of those balancin' scales, or like tunin' a guitar. First you go a little over one way, then you go a little over the other. A little high and a little low. A little left and a little right. Finally, you hit the right weight, or the right note. You find your center of gravity. You get your balance. That's different from doin' the hula."

"Okay, okay. I got it." Slug could rub a thing in worse than Nick Cutter.

"After you get your balance, you want to limber your shoulders. That's all. Now, try it again."

I learned one thing about Slug. He talked a lot. He explained the same thing about fifty different ways.

First something was like weighing yourself on a balancing scale. Then it was like tuning a guitar. Sometimes the first explanation didn't work, but then the third or fourth one did. Anyway, by the time Slug was through, I always knew what he meant.

So I got into my batting position, and Slug pitched the ball. Then I slowed everything down, just the way Slug taught me to do in right field. It was a perfect pitch. I watched the ball till it hung in midair out in front of me. Like it was waiting for my bat. Then I shut my eyes, swung with my whole body, and imagined the treetops where I knew I was sending that baseball. Bye-bye, baby!

Crack! I waited for the sound. *Crack!* I braced myself for the solid shock of bat meeting ball. *Swoosh!* My bat fanned the breeze. I landed on my back in a cloud of dust.

As the dust cleared, I saw Slug's face staring down at me. He was holding his sides laughing.

"Why, boy, you'd make a fine ballet dancer, but that ain't no way to hit a baseball."

"What are you talking about?" I was mad. Not even Slug Smith was going to call me a ballet dancer.

"I'm talking about this: If you're tryin' to hit that baseball, and not just out here doin' ballet turns, you got to keep your eye on the ball."

"But I did watch the ball," I sputtered. "I slowed it down and watched it till it hung out there —"

"That's right. And then you counted your chickens before they hatched. Didn't you?"

"I what?"

"You shut your eyes and started countin' home runs over the trees."

I nodded my head and stared sorrowfully at the ground. Slug was right.

"Now look what I've done." Slug rolled his eyes. "Hurt the kid's feelin's again." Slug stopped for a minute and sighed. "Listen, boy, the point I'm tryin' to make is this: The minute you take your eyes off that ball, you might as well be standin' at the plate doin' ballet turns. 'Cause you just ain't goin' to hit a ball that you don't see."

24

After a few days, Dad and Barbara stopped asking where I went every morning. I think they were glad to have a little more time together. I always took a book with me. But it wasn't until nighttime when I was in bed that I finished *Kidnapped* and started *The Call of the Wild*. After supper, Dad and I discussed my reading. I never saw Wendy anymore except at dinner. Everyone seemed satisfied. There was only one problem. Every night, as I walked home from Slug's, I had a creepy feeling that someone was watching me.

Slug and I met for baseball practice every day. Once we went to God's Country for root beer floats, but mostly, we trained. And don't get me wrong; it was fun, but it was hard.

I've noticed something about people who don't have kids. Either they bend over backward to treat you like they think they're supposed to treat a kid — which means they treat you like a three-year-old — or they don't seem to notice that you're a kid at all. They just treat you like any other person. Well, Slug Smith definitely didn't notice I was a kid.

Every morning we started with exercises, and each morning the exercises got harder: deep knee bends, sit-ups, pushups, and this stretching stuff that Slug called "yoga." In San Francisco, my mom said she went to yoga every Tuesday evening. But I *know* it wasn't the same thing. The stuff we did that summer hurt like heck. One morning, I got stuck with my left arm halfway up my back, my right hand tucked behind my neck, and my right elbow sticking straight up in the air. I thought I'd be in that position for the rest of my life! Slug called it the "cow." I called it the "pits."

After the exercises, we jogged. Two miles! Give me a break. I was only eleven! By the time we finished jogging, I was ready for bed.

"Okay, man." Slug was rubbing his hands together and bouncing around like someone had just plugged him into a wall socket. I was lying on my back in the grass. I couldn't move. "Let's start."

"Start! What are you talking about? What have we been doing for the last two hours? I'm already finished!"

"You're finished, are you? Do you hear that?" Slug talked to one of the popular trees. "Kid says he's finished." Back to me, "Hey, man, you're not finished. That was just the warm-up."

Now do you see what I mean about Slug not noticing that I was a kid?

Slug and I had been training for over a week when I realized he didn't even know my name. I hadn't no-

ticed until then. He always just called me "kid" or
"boy." And *he* talked so much, I felt like I knew him
really well. Then one morning, he borrowed my glove
to show me something.

"Hey, kid, what's this, anyway?" Slug recognized
his autograph.

"It's my autographed glove. I got it on Autograph
Day at Candlestick. There was a big crowd around
you. I never thought you'd stay to —"

Slug nodded his head. "Those were the days, boy."

"What do you mean, 'were'?" I shot back. "You're
still —"

"Still what?" Slug's eyes got angry and his face froze
over. I bit my lip. "Hey, who's The Root, anyway?
That's not your name, is it?"

My stomach sank. Slug had seen the spot where
my teammates crossed out my name. I'd forgotten all
about it.

"Oh, it's nothing."

"Say, what is your name, anyway? Who's The Root?"

"It's, ah . . ." My mind went blank.

"Is it you? Is The Root your name?"

I nodded. "My nickname." I just couldn't lie.

"What's it short for? Roto-Rooter?" Slug roared.

By that time my cheeks were burning. "Tree roots,"
I blurted.

"Tree roots?" Slug stared at me out of the corner
of his eye. Then he glanced over his right shoulder.
"Did the kid say 'tree roots'?" For a second he struggled to keep a straight face. Then he exploded in
laughter. " 'Cause you freeze, right? 'Cause you grow

roots in the outfield!" He slapped his knee and shook his head. "I love it, boy. I really love it."

But I could already feel the tears leaking down the side of my nose.

"Aw, don't cry, man. Nicknames are great. Take my name —"

But I didn't want to hear it. I was tired of his making fun of me. "It's fine for you. You've got a great nickname. Slug for the great slugger. Slugs 'em out of the ballpark. Go ahead and make fun of me, Slug Smith. I guess it won't be the first time."

"Wait a minute," Slug interrupted. "Take it easy, man. You don't know what you're talkin' about. 'Slug' ain't for 'slugger.' 'Slug' is for 'slug.' "

"I don't get it."

" 'Slug' is for 'slug,' as in slow."

"Slow?" I still didn't get it.

"Yeah. Slow. Like in couldn't-get-to-first-base slow."

Only slowly did it dawn on me.

"You see, Roots, when I was a kid I played baseball with my two older brothers. One was a sprinter and one was a hurdler. I ran like I talk — like I got two left feet. I mean, I was the slowest kid you ever saw. I was so slow my brothers called me 'The slug,' as in 'backyard slug.' And the name stuck. It stuck like glue.

"But I loved baseball, so I just kept playin'. Finally, in high school, my coach told me that if I wanted to play anymore, I'd have to learn to hit home runs. That was the only way I'd have time to get around the bases. So, you see, that's just what I did. After that, everybody thought Slug stood for 'slugger.' But I know what Slug stands for. It stands for 'slug.' "

When Slug finished his story my ears were singing.

"Now, tell me how you got your name."

It took just about the whole morning. I mean, in a way, it's kind of a long story. Starting with the St. Remedius game and then the part where Noel tricked me. I even told Slug about the Seton Hall game. How we lost. What Nick Cutter said. How I decided to come to Wisconsin so I wouldn't be in the rematch. By that time, I even threw in the part about Wendy and Barbara and not wanting to hurt my dad's feelings, and about missing my home in San Francisco and my mom. My stomach was growling when I finished. So we went into Slug's kitchen, and he made some great hamburgers. They were smothered in mushrooms. I don't get it. In Wisconsin, mushrooms taste really good.

"Well, Roots, I think you ought to keep it."

"Keep what?"

Slug looked up at the light fixture. " 'Keep what,' he asks." Then back to me, "Keep your name, boy, that's what. Roots. It's a good name."

"Go on . . ."

"I mean it. Anyway, you'll have to keep it for a while."

"Why?"

" 'Cause that's what I'm gonna call you."

*

It's a funny thing about nicknames. I thought Slug would think I was pretty dumb if he knew my teammates called me "The Root." But it turned out just the opposite. The day I told Slug the story about my nickname was the day he and I became friends.

25

I was coming home from Slug's late one evening. We'd been at the lake for almost a month. Suddenly, I heard a crash behind me on the trail. Something had fallen in the underbrush. I spun around, just in time to see a figure take off toward the shore. It was a person all right. I could see the blue jeans and a striped sweater. Funny thing was, it looked like *my* striped sweater. Something was starting to dawn on me. Something that made me take off after those blue jeans. I was going to solve the mystery of the creepy footsteps once and for all.

The lake was full that summer, high up on its banks. Usually, the trail around the lake was a yard from the water's edge. Last year, it bordered the shore, almost forming a ledge over the water. No one used the lakeside trail, so the path was overgrown. Though I was only a few feet behind the mysterious figure, I couldn't get a good look at it.

I pushed myself to go faster. Whoever it was was a darn good runner. Suddenly, when I'd got within a couple of feet of the person, I tripped over a tree root and fell forward. I bumped into the spy, tumbling both of us off the trail and into six feet of water.

When I surfaced, I found myself staring into Wendy's angry face. She was thrashing around in the water, wearing my sweater. My favorite sweater. It was ruined! I wanted to punch her, but the two of us were too cold and too busy scrambling up the steep, rocky shore.

"What's the big idea?" Wendy said that! We were standing on the trail, dripping wet.

" 'Big idea?' *You've* got *my* sweater on."

"So you knocked me in the lake because I was wearing your sweater? Real smart, Josh. Now you've ruined it."

I couldn't believe my ears. The kid spies on me wearing my own favorite sweater, leads me on a wild chase along the lake ending with us both in the water, and then she makes it sound like my fault. Well, I wasn't buying it.

"Wait a minute," I said. "You've been spying. You've been following me every day. Explain that. Then tell me why you're wearing my sweater."

"I got cold. It was cold hiding in the bushes."

"But why were you hiding?" That was the big question.

Suddenly Wendy started to cry. "Because I hate it up here. I have no friends. There's nothing to do, except watch Mom and Ted have fun. Then you disappeared every day, all day. I knew you'd found something fun to do. I just wanted to find out what it was."

All of a sudden, I felt sorry for Wendy. I guess I knew how she felt.

"I sure was surprised, though, when I saw you playing ball with Slug Smith."

"Slug Smith?" My stomach fell. "How did you know that was Slug Smith?"

"I recognized him, dodo. Everyone knows Slug Smith. He's a national hero."

"Why didn't you say something?"

"He's obviously trying to keep it a secret. What was I going to do, call the newspapers?"

Well, it turned out Wendy wasn't so dumb after all. She was a genuine baseball fan. After ballet, baseball was her favorite sport. She even went to Brewers games! No wonder her pitching was so good!

"But I thought you only read library books and collected baseball cards," she continued. "I thought you were a real drip! Actually, you're getting to be an okay batter."

" 'Okay'? I'm a lot better than you, I'll bet."

"I'm second best on my team."

"Yeah, girl's team."

"No! Wisconsin Little League!"

"Hmm."

"Josh" — even before she asked, I knew what the question would be — "can I come play with you and Slug? I'm really good. Honest."

"I don't know, Wendy." Wendy had such a big mouth. I wasn't sure I could risk it. "Slug really wants to keep this secret. And he doesn't want anyone asking why he's up here."

"Don't worry. I won't ask. I already know why he's up here."

"You do?"

"Sure, dummy. 'Cause his career's almost over. 'Cause he has to retire, and he's afraid he'll flop as a TV announcer. He was terrible during the World Series. He was scared stiff."

"What do you mean? Scared of what?"

"Scared of the microphone, stupid. You know, stage fright."

Now the thing I hated most about Wendy was that she always thought she knew everything. And the thing I hated second most was that she called me stupid. Nobody calls me stupid.

"Wendy, it just wouldn't be right. I can't bring you along. I promised Slug no one would find out."

"But I did find out. Besides, you have to let me come."

"I have to?" I started to laugh. "Now why do I have to?"

"Because if you don't," Wendy smiled smugly, "I'll tell Mom and Ted all about it."

26

I didn't talk to Wendy for the whole hike back to the cabin. All I could think of was that my stepsister was blackmailing me. If I took her to Slug's, he'd think I broke my promise. Even worse, he'd meet my lame relative. It was too embarrassing. But if I didn't take Wendy with me, she'd tell Slug's and my secret to everyone.

It was almost dark by the time Wendy and I rounded the path up to the house.

"They're coming!" Dad was on the front porch with a flashlight. Wendy and I struggled up the hill from the lake, soaking wet. We'd missed dinner. We'd scared Dad and Barbara to death. I didn't have to worry about taking Wendy with me to Slug Smith's after all. Wendy and I were about to be grounded for the rest of the summer.

Suddenly, Wendy grabbed my arm.

"Ted! Ted! Come help us. I think Josh is hurt!"

I couldn't believe my ears. "I'm not hurt."

"Quiet, dummy."

"Hurt?" Dad was running down the path closely followed by Barbara.

"Wendy, honey, are you okay?"

"I'm okay, Mom. Really, I'm okay, thanks to Josh —"

"Kids, what happened?" That was my dad. Everyone was talking at once. Except me.

"Josh . . . Mom, Josh . . . I swear . . . he saved my life. We were playing tag over by the Ahlstroms'. I fell in the lake and Josh dived in after me. He saved me. I swear. But I'm afraid he's hurt —"

"I'm not hurt!" But then I felt a sharp stabbing pain in my shin. "Yeow!"

"You are now," Wendy whispered.

Barbara got us dry clothes while Dad reheated firehouse beans and leftover steak. Did it taste good! We even got to eat on the floor in front of the fireplace. Wendy just sat there talking a mile a minute — about the hike, about the chase, about falling in the lake. The scary part was, none of Wendy's story was exactly a lie.

"Sounds like you two had quite an adventure." Dad wasn't a bit angry about our being late. "The only part I don't understand," he said, "is why Wendy got into trouble in the water. You're a good swimmer, Wendy."

"Good question, Ted." Wendy actually thought about it a while. "I think I just got scared."

"Did your feet get tangled in weeds?" Dad suggested.

"It doesn't really matter, does it, Ted?" Barbara interrupted. "You know, as long as they're safe."

"Right, Mom." Wendy nodded. "And the best part is," she continued, grinning at me over a huge slice of watermelon, "Josh and I are going to play baseball together tomorrow morning. Right, Josh?"

Dad raised his eyebrows. "Sounds like fun. Can I play, too?"

"Ah . . . Dad . . . maybe another time, but not tomorrow . . ."

Dad looked sort of disappointed.

Barbara patted him on the shoulder. "Maybe we should let them alone tomorrow, dear." Then her eyes lit up and she grinned just like Wendy. "Maybe you and I could be alone tomorrow, Ted. We could take a hike!"

Later, Dad popped us some popcorn. Then he and Barbara took their coffee on the deck to watch the stars and listen to the loons. Normally I went out on the deck after dinner, too. Listening to the loons beat listening to Wendy! But that night something was on my mind. Something I wanted to settle with Wendy.

"Doesn't tricking your parents bother you?"

Wendy folded her arms and batted her eyes at me like I was a four-year-old. "Hold it, Josh. Everything I told Mom and Ted was true — except, of course, I exaggerated about your saving my life."

"You know what I mean, Wendy. It really bothers me when I fool my parents. It makes it seem like they're stupid."

127

"Josh, I said don't worry about it. The point is, we're probably not fooling them."

"What do you mean?"

"It's really very simple, Josh," Wendy replied smugly. "If we're happy, they're happy. That's all that counts. Besides, my mom's not stupid. She's an anthropologist."

27

Wendy was happy, all right. She had me right where she wanted me. I, on the other hand, was panicked. What would a National League All-Star think about practicing with my lame stepsister? What a waste of time! Worst of all, there was Wendy's big mouth.

I lay in bed worrying about this most of the night. Finally, I thought of something that allowed me to drift peacefully to sleep. The warm-up! Wendy would never be able to do it! After the warm-up, Wendy would be glad to leave me and Slug alone.

Every day for the past week, it had seemed like Slug was in training. He worked out before I arrived each morning. He fixed a special "training lunch." He talked to himself more and more about "the team." He even bought a special radio so he could tune in to the Giants games. We took a break to listen whenever there was a game.

And every day the warm-up got more difficult. Wendy would be on her way home in ten minutes. And once Wendy actually met Slug Smith, she wouldn't tell our secret. She'd already kept the secret almost as long as I had. All I had to do was explain the situation to Slug. He'd figure out the rest.

The next morning, Wendy and I ate breakfast together and ran out the door at nine-thirty. Boy, did Wendy look happy. So did I. I was finally going to get my revenge.

Wendy was right about Barbara and Dad. They were so happy to see us getting along, they didn't dare ask where we were going.

"Have fun, you two."

"Be careful."

"Get home before dinner."

When we neared the guesthouse, I stopped running.

"These practice sessions are serious business," I told Wendy. "Slug's not fooling around. It's like he's in training."

"Okay, okay."

"You can't embarrass me either."

"I won't. Don't worry."

"No whining if you can't keep up."

"I know, I know."

"Promise?"

"Yes, I promise."

"If you can't keep up, you promise to go home and not tell Dad and Barbara?"

"No problem, Josh. I promise. No problem at all."

Then I ran ahead to talk to Slug. I explained about Wendy spying on us and threatening to tell Barbara and Dad. Slug didn't seem very concerned about our secret anymore. In fact, lately he'd even stopped wearing his baseball cap when we went into town. And he always wore a Giants T-shirt. I almost wondered if he wanted people to recognize him.

I also explained about the warm-up.

At first, Slug frowned. "Are you sure you know what you're doin', Roots?" he asked skeptically.

I nodded.

Then Slug grinned, rubbing his hands together. "Okay, kid. You asked for it, you got it!"

I could tell that day's warm-up was going to be a killer!

Every morning I'd done thirty pushups. That morning I did forty. Wendy did fifty. Every morning I'd done twenty sit-ups. That morning I did thirty. Wendy did thirty-five. Every morning I'd done three pull-ups. That morning I did four. Wendy did five. Wendy and Slug jogged three miles. I jogged two and a half. Wendy didn't run home after ten minutes.

"This is nothing compared to my ballet exercises." Wendy had just finished jogging and was barely out of breath.

I was lying in the grass with a cramp in my leg.

"You know, your stepsister's actually one heck of a little athlete."

Wendy beamed.

"Thanks, Slug," I moaned. That was all I needed to hear.

For the next three hours, Wendy batted a thousand. I couldn't seem to get my glove on the ball.

28

Wendy and I trained at Slug's every morning that week. In fact, we all got to be friends. It's hard to believe, but Wendy and I did end up having a lot in common. After all, we both liked the Brewers. And since I had to have a stepsister, at least she was a darn good baseball player. So what if she could do more pushups than I could?

It turned out Wendy and I also liked the same movies and some of the same music. I even let her listen to my U2 tapes. And I found out Wendy and I had both been worried about having new relatives. I couldn't believe it. Wendy had been as nervous about meeting me as I'd been about meeting her! Of course, it took a while to find this out. In the end, though, I think the best thing that Wendy and I had in common was that we were both Slug's friend. Slug told me I was lucky. He said my stepsister is cool.

When we weren't training, Slug and Wendy and I listened to Giants games. And any other baseball game that was on. It was the middle of August, and the

Giants were only a half game out of first place. By that time, Slug had shaved his beard and mustache. He looked like his old self. He even sounded like his old self. All he could talk about was baseball.

Dad couldn't believe that Wendy and I were getting along so well. Every time he started to mention it, though, Barbara changed the subject. Wendy is right; Barbara is pretty smart after all. Lucky for us. That way we had no trouble keeping Slug's secret.

Glove up. Glove down. Visor up. Get behind the ball. The training at Slug's got more intense every day. Batting was just as bad. Feet apart. Shoulder back. Chin up. Watch the ball. Keep your bat up. Get your shoulder into it. There were always a thousand things to remember. I couldn't seem to remember any of them.

Finally one day, I threw my glove down. It was no use. I was back where I had started. "I'll never get it all. I'm no good. I give up."

For the first time, Slug didn't make fun of me. Instead, he walked up beside me and put his arm around my shoulder.

"I think I know how you feel, kid. But you can't look at it that way. It's getting better. Believe me. You just have to keep taking it one step at a time."

"How?"

"Roots, I've been learnin' a lot teachin' you base-ball." Slug gazed past me. It was like he was talking to someone else again. "I've been thinkin' about this all week. Baseball's no different from anything else.

It's like life. You can't look at it all at once. It's too scary. There's too much you don't know. Too much you can't do."

I sat down wearily on the grass. Slug sat down beside me.

"What do you mean?" Even Wendy stopped her sit-ups and joined us.

"Let me see if I can explain it. It's like . . ." Slug thought for a minute. "It's like goin' to my aunt Polly's for dinner."

I smiled and shook my head. I could tell this was going to be a good one.

"See, every Christmas when I was a kid we drove down to St. Louis for dinner at my aunt Polly's. She made the best food. Baked ham and redeye gravy, and corn, and sweet potatoes, mashed potatoes, biscuits, and peas. There were three kinds of pie, and there was homemade ice cream for dessert. And every year, Dad said, 'No presents till you eat all your dinner. Otherwise you'll hurt your aunt Polly's feelings. She'll think you don't like her cookin'.'

"But every year, it got so I dreaded that Christmas dinner more and more. Because by the time I sat down at Aunt Polly's table and saw my plate piled high with food — why, I practically got sick. I couldn't eat a bite!

"My mom was dead. Aunt Polly was just about my favorite person in the whole world. I didn't want to hurt her feelin's. And I did want to open my Christmas presents. But there was no way I could eat that dinner.

"All the other kids had dessert and started openin'

134

presents. Finally I just sat there alone with the grown-ups. First Cousin Ethelda told me to eat so I'd get big. That didn't work. Then Uncle Harry told me to eat so I could make my Papa happy. But that didn't work either. Finally my aunt Polly sent everybody else away from the table. The two of us just sat there a while, starin' at each other. Then all of a sudden, I started to cry.

" 'It's not that I don't like your cookin', Aunt Polly. It's just that I lost my appetite.'

" 'I understand, Rodney,' she said. Rodney is my given name, so you can see why I like nicknames. 'But your problem is that you're lookin' at the whole plate at once.'

" 'Huh?' I said. 'How else do you look at a plate?'

" 'You see,' she continued, 'if you look at the whole plate at once, it'll scare you. There's too much. You've got to take it in a little at a time. Slowly. Start on the peas. There aren't too many of those. Then work on the ham. Try to finish it. Then eat the potatoes. Eat slowly. Do the best you can. I know you like the food. There's just too much. Then, when you can't do any more, go tell your papa. Tell him you tried. He'll understand. He'll understand if you tell him you tried, and you show him how much you've done.'

"So that's what I did. Aunt Polly and I just sat there talkin' and eatin'. The more I ate, the more my appetite came back. A little at a time. Well, before I knew it, I'd finished the whole dinner.

"I never forgot that dinner with Aunt Polly. She was like a mother to me. I still kind of talk to her now and then. Like she's around somewhere and can hear me."

I stood up, not entirely sure I understood the point of the story.

Wendy sat nodding her head up and down real fast. "I get it. I see what you mean. It's like slowing the ball down in baseball. Breaking things down. Learning the steps for how to bat or how to catch. It's scary otherwise. You watch that ball come at you a hundred miles an hour, and you know it could knock all your teeth out."

"Right."

"There's just one thing I don't understand, then," Wendy continued.

"What's that?"

"How come you can explain everything so clearly to us here, but you can't talk in front of the micro-phone on TV? You were terrible during the World Series."

I almost threw up. Wendy's big mouth had done it again! I wanted the ground to open up and swallow me.

But instead of getting mad, Slug just shook his head.

"Forget it, kid. I'm no good at explainin' things on TV. I talk too much and I talk too slow. See, when you've got a microphone in front of your face on TV, it ain't like jivin' with reporters in the locker room. As a sportscaster, you've got about twenty seconds to explain why some club just lost the game. I can't say my full name in twenty seconds. First, I start sweatin'.

136

My make-up runs. Then, I trip over my words. Then my mind plain goes blank. I freeze."

"Well," Wendy persisted. My jaw fell open. No other kid in the entire world would dare give Slug Smith advice. "Josh and I know you're good at explaining things. If you can't do it on TV, maybe it's just because you haven't learned how yet. Like Josh being afraid of catching the baseball."

Thanks a lot.

"Maybe you just shouldn't think about it all together. Maybe there's a way to learn to be a broadcaster the way you learned to be a baseball hero — just one step at a time."

Slug grinned. "You know, I been thinkin' about that, too. I've got a whole year before I have to retire. In the off-season, I could start learnin' how to talk on TV."

"Sure you could," Wendy and I chimed in together. "You'll be great!"

29

One morning — it was the Monday of our last week at the lake — Wendy and I arrived at Slug's as usual. He wasn't in the meadow, and he wasn't at the dock. He wasn't in the guesthouse. We were about to knock on the cabin door, when we heard his voice. At first, I thought he was talking to Aunt Polly. Then we realized Slug was on the phone.

"What difference does it make where Turtle Lake is?" we heard him shout.

Silence.

"It's north of Madison. Look it up on the map. Better yet, let the *Chronicle* look it up on the map."

Silence.

"Am I in the startin' line-up Friday, or not?"

Silence.

"Of course I'm in shape. There's nothin' else to do up here."

Silence.

"That's right, Roger. Half game out, you *don't* have a choice."

Wendy and I knew we shouldn't be listening, so

we turned and left. When we were halfway down Arrowhead Trail, we heard a long, loud "whoop" echo off of the Ahlstroms' dock.

Wendy and I returned to Slug's house the next morning. Again, Slug wasn't in the meadow, and he wasn't at the dock. We knocked loudly on his door, but there was no answer. I worried he'd moved already. Wendy was sure he wouldn't leave without saying good-bye. As we turned sadly home, the door to the garage slammed. Slug walked out carrying two big suitcases.

"Where're you going?" As if Wendy and I had to ask.

"I'll tell you where I'm goin'." Slug was grinning from ear to ear. "I'm goin' home! And I don't mean Milwaukee. I'm goin' back to San Francisco to play baseball. And if the Giants are goin' to have any chance at the World Series, I'd better get there fast!"

"You're really going to play baseball again?" Wendy and I both shouted at once.

"I'm not much good at anything else, now am I? Not yet, that is. I'm packin' my bags and flyin' home tomorrow." Slug stopped and stared at me for a minute. "I'd have left today, but I thought I might talk you into flyin' home with me."

"Could I?" The thought of it made me dizzy. But as quickly, my heart sank. "I can't, Slug. I mean, I'd like to, but I'm supposed to spend the year here. I promised my dad — "

"But you don't really want to be here," said Slug.

"And your dad won't be happy if you're not happy," said Wendy.

"No, but —"

"Well, tell him, then, Roots." Slug looked over his shoulder. For a minute, I thought I could see Aunt Polly. "Roger about bites my head off and threatens to fire me, and Roots here is afraid to talk to his own father. What's the matter with the boy?" Then he turned back to me. "If my manager can understand a fellow changin' his mind, then I'll bet your dad can understand, too, Roots."

Well, I didn't talk to my dad that night. And I didn't leave with Slug the next day. Of course, I dreamed about it. All that night. But that's only the way movies end.

Instead, that evening, Slug stopped by our house to say good-bye to me and Wendy. Dad sure was surprised to find out who our weird next-door neighbor was! But Slug had put on a fancy jacket and tie. He didn't look a bit weird. He looked cool! First he introduced himself to Barbara and my dad. Then Slug got that angry look in his eyes again.

"I guess I'll just never figure out how you could think *I* was weird," he said to my dad.

I've never seen my dad get so red. He sputtered and stammered. Then he offered to drive Slug to the little airport at Twin Falls.

Early the next morning, Dad, Barbara, Wendy, and I drove Slug Smith to meet his plane. In one way, it

140

was really exciting. Kind of like a dream come true. There I was, driving the Giants' star batter back to rejoin his team. Slug's whereabouts wasn't even a secret anymore. His manager had called the newspapers.

But in another way, it was kind of sad. Once Slug was a national hero again, he wasn't going to pal around with a kid like me. Face it. When Slug walked up the gangway, he would walk out of my life forever.

When we got to the tiny waiting area at the airport, I was so busy getting sad, I didn't notice the unusually big crowd gathered there. In fact, it wasn't until four flash bulbs popped in my face that I realized Gate 2 was jammed with reporters and cameramen.

"Slug!"

"Mr. Smith?"

"Hey, Slugger!"

The name echoed from every corner of the room.

"Are you coming out of retirement?"

"Just what is Turtle Lake?"

"Do you plan to play in tomorrow's game?"

The questions popped as fast as the flash bulbs. Finally, someone with a minicam shoved a microphone in front of Slug's mouth.

"Could you tell us, Slug, just why you went into hiding?"

Slug was standing right next to me. The question hit him like a line drive, screaming a hundred miles an hour. The whole waiting room fell silent. For a full minute we waited for Slug Smith to answer. Then I saw his muscles slowly relax.

"I guess I quit cause I . . . I was . . . well . . ." Sud-

141

denly Slug grinned. "You might say 'cause I started lookin' at the whole plate at once."

"Huh?" That reporter backed off shaking his head.

But a woman immediately shoved her way into his place, and jammed another mike in Slug's face. I recognized her. She was Debra Cole from KSAP.

"Can you tell us who your friend is, Slug?"

All of a sudden, I noticed that the tiny red light on the minicam was pointing straight at *me*. Slug jabbed me in the ribs.

"Smile, boy. You're on TV."

When I saw myself later that night on the evening news, I couldn't believe my eyes. Not only didn't I smile, I didn't even close my mouth. It hung wide open while the camera shot a close-up of my molars. It was gross. Then the camera swung back to Slug.

"This here is my training partner, Roots."

"Did you say Roots, Slug?" Debra Cole asked.

"Yeah. Roots," Slug repeated. "His teammates call him Roots 'cause he's such a great kid. Everybody roots for him!"

30

My teammates in San Francisco must have seen that newscast, too. The next evening the phone rang. It was Nick Cutter.

"Uh . . . ah, Josh? I mean, ah . . . Roots?"

"Yeah?"

"I saw you on TV last night. That was —"

I waited for him to make some crack about my molars.

"— awesome!"

"What?"

"Awesome. Like radical, Roots. I didn't know you were training with Slug Smith all summer."

"It was kind of a secret."

"Um, Roots, I hate to bother you, but . . . the reason I'm calling is, see, the rest of the Tigers and I wanted . . . We want to know if there's any chance . . . Would you be on our team again this year? We already asked Bobby. He promised to save your position . . ."

"Who was that, Josh?" Dad saw me hang up the

phone. I didn't even say good-bye. "Is everything okay?"

I was too confused to answer. I ran upstairs to my room and lay down on my bed. I didn't even have dinner!

Sleeping has never been a problem for me. Most nights I fall asleep the second my head hits the pillow. But that night was different. Thoughts switched on and off in my brain like buzzers. The strange part was that it wasn't just one, big, bad thought that was keeping me awake. Every once in a while, that happens. I have nightmares. Like the night, at home in San Francisco, when I was sure a wolf was hiding in my bathroom.

But this wasn't that kind of a thought. It was a crowd of thoughts in my brain. And they weren't bad thoughts. They were thoughts about Slug and Wendy. About baseball, and the Seton Hall game. About vacations, my mother, my room, my school, Danny Guidi, and Nick Cutter.

Only one thought came back over and over. That was "home." Summer was over and I wasn't going home. I thought about Dad and Barbara and Wendy. I'd tried to imagine what it would be like living with them all year. But every time, my mind changed the subject. It thought about home. I'd tried to imagine a new school, making new friends, never seeing Nick Cutter again. But still my mind changed the subject. It thought about home. On and off. On and off. Like blinkers in my brain. There was no way I could sleep.

Then I found myself remembering Slug's story about

Christmas dinner. I hadn't understood the story when Slug told it. But suddenly I knew just what he meant. A whole jumble of things was happening to me. The problem wasn't that they were bad things. The problem was that there were too many. Then I heard Aunt Polly: "There's too much. It'll scare you. You've got to take it in a little at a time."

Like a line drive, I had to slow things down. So for the next half hour, I lay in bed slowing everything down. When I finished, I'd realized two important things. First, that I liked my new family, and I didn't want to hurt their feelings. Second, that I really did want to go home. The next thing I knew, I was fast asleep.

Parents really are unpredictable. Dad's feelings weren't hurt much at all when I told him I wanted to go home to San Francisco. Maybe that's because first, I told him how much I love him. Then I explained about my friends and my baseball team. I even told him the story about my nickname. I think Dad understood why I wanted to go home.

We decided I'd stay in California for seventh and eighth grades, and plan to spend ninth grade in Wisconsin. In the meantime, I'd visit Dad over Christmas and Easter. We even decided to have Wendy visit me in San Francisco at Thanksgiving. I couldn't wait to introduce her to my friends. In a way, I guess Dad was right. Wendy and I are a lot alike.

And then, before I knew it, my plane landed in San

Francisco, and my mom was hugging me and complaining about my hair being too short. It was as if I'd never left. She said that twenty people phoned her the night I was on TV. And you know what? My own mother didn't even see me! She'd turned off the news before they did sports! Well, I guess that'll teach her.

31

The morning of the Seton Hall rematch, I woke up at five-thirty. First I paced around my room. Then I tried on my uniform, just to make sure I had everything: shirt, pants, socks, stirrups, cleats, cap, glove. There's a lot to remember. Mom made me a big breakfast, but I was too nervous to eat. Instead, I walked to the Guidis' house. It was seven-thirty by that time. I sat in the kitchen with Nonni.

School hadn't opened yet, so the game was scheduled for twelve-thirty. At eleven-thirty I phoned Bobby, our coach, just to make sure of the time.

At twelve-thirty, the whole Tiger team assembled on the field of Applegate Playground. As we listened to Bobby's last-minute instructions, I checked out the stands. Danny was sitting with Jenny Sinton right behind the Tigers' bench. Jenny waved at me. I saw my mom in the fourth row. I waved at her, but she didn't see me. She was too busy looking around, like she was expecting someone.

Then I saw a tall, dark figure stroll up the path along the third-base line of the baseball diamond.

Whoever it was had a baseball cap pulled down over his eyes. He climbed the bleachers, stopped, and turned around like he was looking for someone. Then do you know what he did? He sat down in the seat next to my mother! And when the person took off his hat, do you know who it was? Slug Smith!

Well, the story doesn't end like a movie. I could tell you I was the hero that day. That I hit a grand slam in the bottom of the sixth and won the game for my school. I could tell you my teammates carried me off the field, and that Bobby presented me with the MVP award. I could tell you that, but I won't. That's not what happened.

Instead, I batted two for three. One single and one double. Nick Cutter did hit a grand slam in the fourth. At the bottom of the sixth, the Tigers led by two runs. Seton Hall was up, and Brian McMonagle stood at the plate. There were two outs, a man on second, and a man on third. I'd been watching Brian all afternoon. He's Seton Hall's best player. He always points his left foot to right field when he bats. He leans into the ball and, if it's outside and he gets a lot of wood on it, the ball sails straight to right field.

The first pitch was a strike. The second a foul tip. But the third pitch hung a little outside. Brian connected just before the ball crossed the plate. Crack! I heard that clean, sharp sound of wood on leather. Crack! The unmistakable sound of a solid hit. Then I watched the hard, white bullet shoot straight at Nick Cutter's head. If it hit him, he was dead. Nick bit the dust. That's right, he ducked. I had advanced to just where I knew the ball was heading. I raised my glove. The sun was in my eyes. I used my glove to block it. Then the world clicked into slow motion, and the baseball just floated toward me. You know, I had all the time in the world to reach up and pluck it out of the sky.

FINAL SCORE: TIGERS   9
                           SETON HALL   7